F-M   Conwell, Kent
Con   The Crystal Skull
       Murders

Tony Boudreaux Mystery

THE CRYSTAL SKULL MURDERS

A Tony Boudreaux Mystery

The *Tony Boudreaux Mystery* series:

Death in the French Quarter
The Swamps of Bayou Teche
Extracurricular Murder
The Ying On Triad
Death in the Distillery
Skeletons of the Atchafalaya
Galveston
Vicksburg

Other Mysteries by Kent Conwell:

The Riddle of Mystery Inn

THE CRYSTAL SKULL MURDERS

•

Kent Conwell

AVALON BOOKS
NEW YORK

Published by Thomas Bouregy & Co., Inc.
160 Madison Avenue, New York, NY 10016

Library of Congress Cataloging-in-Publication Data

Conwell, Kent.
    The crystal skull murders / Kent Conwell.
        p. cm.
    ISBN: 978-0-8034-9898-3 (acid-free paper)   1. Private in-
vestigators—Texas—Austin—Fiction.   2. Austin (Tex.)—Fiction.   3. Murder—Investigation—Fiction.   I. Title.

    PS3553.O547C79   2008
    813'.54—dc22   2007047385

PRINTED IN THE UNITED STATES OF AMERICA
ON ACID-FREE PAPER
BY HADDON CRAFTSMEN, BLOOMSBURG, PENNSYLVANIA

To Rhet and Ryan—I hope you have as much fun figuring this one out as I had writing it. And to my wife, Gayle.

Chapter One

If someone had asked me what a chauvinistic female, a dead wino, a torched hip-hop bar, a crystal skull, and five million dollars had in common, I would have answered absolutely nothing!

As usual, I was wrong. They spelled out big-time trouble for me.

And trouble is exactly what slapped me in the face when my boss, Marty Blevins, called me into his office on the first Monday of autumn.

Sitting in one of the two chairs in front of his battered desk with her back to me was a woman whose black hair draped over the shoulders of her black business suit.

Although it was only 9:30 on that September 25, two days after autumn ushered in a welcome cool front, a sheen of sweat glistened on Marty's rotund face. As usual, he wore a rumpled suit of tan linen. As usual, his garish tie was loosened. As usual, his collar was unbuttoned—typical Marty Blevins, owner of Blevins' Investigations, my humble home for the last several years.

He grinned up at me. "Tony. Meet Doreen Patterson. She's coming over to us from Texas State Investigations. Doreen, this is Tony Boudreaux."

Doreen rose and faced me somberly. She offered her hand and with a tone as grim as the expression on her face, said, "Mister Boudreaux."

A chill ran down my spine. Level with mine, her black eyes, made even larger by black eyelashes, seemed lifeless. She wore little makeup, and her dark-red lipstick covered about half of her full lips. I took her hand and nodded. "Miss Patterson." Her flesh was cool. I glanced at Marty, wondering what he was up to. Surely, he hadn't invited me in just to meet Miss Congeniality.

She promptly corrected me with a sharp tone reminiscent of the nuns back in elementary school. "Ms. Patterson, if you don't mind."

My ears burned. I glanced sidelong at Marty who was wearing an insipid grin I would have loved to wipe off his face. "Excuse me, Ms. Patterson."

Marty continued. "Sit down, both of you. Tony, I called you in for two reasons. First, you remember that guy whose bar burned down on Sixth Street last week? You know, the one who was sent to us by that woman in Lafayette."

"Yeah. Getdown Joe Sillery. Hip-Hop Bar and Grill. Fawn Williams sent him to us. What about him?"

A sly grin curled his fat lips. "He offered a fat fee for us to find who torched his place."

I frowned. "What about the cops? That's their job."

Marty's grin grew wider. "They already figured the old wino they found dead was the one who set it."

I stiffened. I knew many of the moochers who ran the streets in downtown Austin. Despite my inexperience, early in my PI career, I recognized Sixth Street as the birthplace of devious dodges, unscrupulous schemes, and crooked conspiracies. Once the winos, invisible denizens of the seamy underside of Sixth Street, learned I would pay for legitimate tips, I developed my own little network of undesirables who often came up with desirable information. "Wino? I didn't read about that."

He waved his hand and smiled in what he considered his most charming manner at his new hire. "It wasn't mentioned. You know the media."

I felt Ms. Doreen Patterson watching me, but I ignored her. A fist of anxiety knotted in my stomach as I wondered if the dead man might be one of my old homeless bums who called the alleys and dumpsters of Sixth Street home-sweet-home. "They know who he was?"

"Naw." Marty shook his head. "Just another drunken wino."

Marty's compassion never ceased to amaze me. Personally, I felt a kindred relationship to those poor slobs;

for more than once, I'd run across my old man down on Sixth Street bumming for loose change.

Where he was now, I had no idea except that one day, if he didn't fall under one of the trains he was hopping, he'd be back. "So, if the cops think the old man torched it, why is Getdown paying us?"

"He doesn't believe the wino did it. According to him, he'd turned down a few offers from some important people."

"And he thinks this might be their way of suggesting he rethink his decision, huh?"

"Yeah, that's what he figures."

"So, what kind of fee is he paying?"

"A big one. Five thousand retainer. Another five if we find who torched the place. You should be able to take care of it in a week or so. What do you think?"

I glanced at Doreen whose expression was still as dour as when I met her. I was beginning to wonder if she might be suffering from some kind of genetic or psychosomatic facial paralysis. "Yeah, I'd say so. A week. Interview Getdown. See what he thinks, then contact the others, but you know," I added. "If it was torched, any names he gives us will have alibis tighter than a fat woman's girdle." I grimaced as soon as the words burst from my overloaded mouth. My ears burned. "Sorry, Ms. Patterson. I—"

She looked at me coolly, her black eyes cold and hard. A wry grin twisted her lips. "Never mind."

I rose from my chair. "Okay, Marty. I'll get right on

it." I nodded to Doreen Patterson and told my first lie of the day. "It was nice to meet you, Ms. Patterson, and please excuse my bad manners."

Marty stopped me. "Hold on, Tony. I'm not finished."

I looked around at him, puzzled. "What now?"

"Doreen. What with you being an ex-schoolteacher, I figured you'd be the one on the staff best qualified to mentor Doreen for the first few weeks. You know, sort of break her in to our way of doing business." He paused and turned to Doreen. "What do you know about arson?"

"Not much, Marty, but I learn fast, very fast. You won't have to worry about that." She looked around at me.

Marty grinned. I frowned. The two of them were on a first name basis, but she insisted I call her Ms. Patterson. Why the difference, or had I missed something?

Chapter Two

When I had climbed out of bed that morning and retrieved the paper from the porch, I reveled in the nip of the early morning air. Behind me, a cat meowed. I glanced around as A.B. paused in the open door. "Looks like it's going to be a beautiful day, little fella."

I drew a lungful of cool air into my lungs. A couple days earlier, autumn greeted us with the first cool front of the season, a welcome respite from the blazing Texas sun. The cool air hung around. I squatted and scratched the back of A.B.'s neck. "Like they say, all's right with the world, huh?"

The little guy couldn't argue. All had been right with his world ever since that day I plucked him from the grasp of two swamp Neanderthals who were planning on sticking him on a hook and using him for alligator bait. That's how he came up with his moniker, A.B.

And now, three hours later as I walked back to my desk with Doreen Patterson tailing me, I couldn't believe just how a beautiful day that had started off so well could have gone south so fast.

"So, where do we start?" she asked as she slipped into the chair in front of my desk. She eyed the clutter on my desk distastefully, and I knew instantly she was one of those super-organized people who deemed it their mission in life that not a hair, not a slip of paper, or not even a thought should be out of place.

"First, some preliminary legwork." I reached for the phone and punched in number for Bob Ray Burrus, an old friend who worked the evidence room at the downtown police station.

He answered on the third ring. After we exchanged greetings and swore in blood that we would get together soon, I asked if the dead man outside the Hip-Hop had been ID'ed.

"You mean the old wino?"

"Yeah."

"Naw, not as far as I know. From what I picked up around here, he got whopped on the head and hemorrhaged." I grimaced, and he continued. "What's going on? I thought the fire was pretty well wrapped up."

"The owner isn't convinced the old man torched the place. Is the department looking into the old guy's death?"

"Got to, but—you know how it goes. Wino, no one knows who he was or where he was from. Not really a priority."

"Yeah, yeah, I know."

"Well, if you find out who he was, let us know, okay?"

I played innocent. "How could I find out?"

"Come on, Tony. You know that bunch of derelicts down there better than anyone. After all, your old man—" He hesitated, then apologetically muttered. "Well, you know what I mean."

I laughed. "Hey, no problem. I'll always appreciate you calling me that time he got booked down there."

"Anytime. Take care."

Replacing the receiver, I thumbed through the directory for Getdown Joe Sillery's number but came up empty. "That's about what I expected," I muttered, hanging up and pushing back from my desk. I shook my head and grinned at Doreen who was watching me with an expressionless face. "Sometimes I wish I'd taken up bull-fighting instead of PI work. Not nearly the hassle. Let's go."

She rose smoothly and headed for the door. "Not me. This is the kind of job I was born for."

I had expected a little lighthearted bantering, but all I got in return was a somber response. I shrugged it off. If she wanted it all to be business, that was fine with me.

Neither of us spoke as we rode the elevator down to

the first floor. Outside, I headed to my Chevrolet Silverado pickup, a gift with all the frills from Jack Edney for making him a multimillionaire when I uncovered the family member who murdered his father. "Hop in," I said. "We're going downtown."

She jerked to a halt and stared at me as if I were a first cousin to the Cyclops. "In this?" Her tone was filled with disbelief. "A pickup?"

I paused with my hand on the door handle and stared across the hood at her.

She eyed me defiantly. "I don't ride in pickups. I hate pickups."

All I could do was shake my head in wonder. A Texas woman who didn't like pickups! I said to myself, *Marty, you dumb tub of lard, what have you gotten us into with this woman?* I shrugged and opened the door. "Your choice. Ride or walk."

A smug smile played over her lips. She pointed to a cherry red Jaguar XK roadster. "I'll follow you," she said, turning on her heel.

"Hey!"

She stopped and looked around, her brow knit, probably in surprise that I had the effrontery to shout at her.

Nodding to her Jag, I said, "You might not want to take a car like that down where we're going."

A smug smile played over her lips. "Don't worry about me. I know what I'm doing."

I shook my head and glanced up at the office window. Marty was watching. I held my hands out to the side as if to say now what? He shook his head, and I climbed in my pickup. I tried to warn her.

*   *   *

Our office on Lamar was only a few blocks from Sixth Street. Normally I drive too fast, but I took it easy so she could stay with me, although I was tempted to take a route through some of the higher density traffic areas just to make her sweat. But the old Southern chivalry in me prevailed.

At ten-thirty in the morning, Sixth Street is struggling to awaken itself from the previous night's celebrations. Gone is the raucous, rowdy, and riotous revelry that animated the street only hours earlier.

Sixth Street was opening its eyes to its daily hangover—subdued, contrite, and penitent. Like bleary eyes slowly opening against the bright light of morning, doors swung open up and down the street, signaling to the early morning boozers the shops were once again open for business.

As I turned onto Sixth, I began searching the almost empty sidewalks for my local winos, hoping the dead man was not one of them. *Yet*, I reminded myself, *I knew them all. Who else could it be?*

S. S. Thibeaux, a rail-thin black man from Vernon Parish on the Sabine River, shuffled out of Neon Larry's Bar and Grill as we passed. He waved. I waved back.

Moments later, I pulled in at the curb down the street from the Hip-Hop, which was now only charred brick walls standing guard over mounds of sodden charcoal. In the rear there were the blackened remains of a hallway across which ran outdated steam pipes about five feet above the ground. Jimmy's Bistro next door was closed down, having been damaged by the fire and water.

Doreen pulled in behind my pickup.

I climbed out and shut the door.

She came to stand beside me. With a curl to her lip, she stared at the hulk that was once a hangout for wannabe hip-hoppers. "It's a mess," she observed.

With a crooked grin, I quipped. "You should have seen it before the fire."

She looked up at me wearily, obviously not impressed by my levity.

Two doors down, Buck Topper threw open the door of the Red Rabbit and paused in the middle of the sidewalk, looking up and down the street. He was one of those bony sorts whose chest sagged into his belly. Although I had known Buck for a few years, and he was always amiable, I was still uncomfortable around him. Maybe it was because he considered himself a ladies' man or maybe because he had shifty eyes or maybe because he never brushed his teeth. I would have sworn the life forms growing between his teeth were first cousins to what I sometimes found growing in the back of my refrigerator.

He grinned when he spotted me, revealing two missing front teeth, one up, one down. "Hey, Tony. Getting an early start?" He eyed Doreen curiously.

"You know me, Buck. I'm a good little AA'er." Remembering my manners, I turned to Doreen. "This is

Buck Topper. He owns the Red Rabbit. Buck, meet Doreen Patterson—newest member on the staff of Blevins' Investigation."

Buck leered. "Glad to meet you, Doreen."

Departing from her trademark growls, she replied in honeyed tones. "Same here, Buck."

Buck grinned sappily at me.

I rolled my eyes. I didn't know Doreen well, but the transition from her growling and snarling to words dripping with magnolia blossoms told me that she was playing games with Buck. "I'm looking for Getdown. Seen him around?"

He shook his head. "Not since last night. He said he was coming back this morning." He cut his eyes at Doreen and grinned. "He usually comes in for a bite since his placed burned down."

Her expression remained unchanged, sort of what you might call a sterile "come hither."

I glanced around. "What about Downtown or Goofy-foot? Seen either of them around?"

"Naw." A frown knit his brows, and he scratched his armpit. "Funny. I ain't seen much of the bunch since the fire. I kinda figured they'd hit me up the next few days, but the only one that come in was Goofyfoot."

Gesturing to the closed bar between the Hip-Hop and the Red Rabbit, I said, "Looks like Jimmy's Bistro picked up some damage. What about your place?"

He shook his head. "Nothing to worry about, but you're right about the Bistro. Calvin closed it down.

Looks like they're going to have to tear both down." He paused, then added. "If I could handle what Getdown and Calvin want for their places, I could build me a right profitable little business here. Dress up the place. Even down to fancy green and yellow uniforms for my people like Getdown. I might do the uniforms anyway."

I shrugged. "Calvin couldn't be asking that much. In fact, I don't know how he stayed open. I never saw more than a dozen or so customers in there at one time."

Buck grinned slyly. "Well, there's customers, and then there are customers."

Doreen frowned at me.

"You talking drugs, Buck?"

"Hey, all I hear is talk."

I filed that little nugget of information away in the back of my head. Pointing to the rear of the Hip-Hop, I asked, "Goofyfoot still hang out in the alley?"

Buck shrugged. "Probably."

"Well, I suppose we'll go take a look."

He smiled at Doreen again and, without taking his eyes off her, added, "Why don't you two come in for some coffee before you go?" He brushed his shiny black hair back over his ears.

Before I could reply, Doreen said, "No, thanks, but you can do me a favor, Buck."

His face lit up. "Sure, Doreen. Just you name it, honey."

She gestured to her Jag. "While Tony and I are gone, would you keep an eye on my car?"

"You bet," he gushed.

She turned to me and, with a smug grin on her face, said. "I'm ready if you are."

If I'd been with anyone else after we left Buck, we would have joked how Doreen had managed to play Buck like a game of Monopoly. After all, when I suggested she didn't want to take an expensive car like the Jag down to Sixth Street, she had promptly informed me she knew what she was doing.

Obviously, she did.

Doreen, one; Tony, zero.

Chapter Three

She wrinkled her nose at the garbage filling the alley. "What's back here?"

"This is where some of the street guys live."

She curled the side of her lip. "Winos? What do we need them for?" The tone in her voice revealed her obvious disgust for street bums.

I studied her for several moments, saying nothing.

She frowned. "What?"

In my four plus decades on this earth, I'd worked with many people whom I would never invite to a backyard barbecue, but I'd always managed to find a way to channel my efforts so that usually we succeeded in whatever undertaking we faced.

This was no different. I cleared my throat. "You're really interested in this PI business, huh?"

Her frown deepened as if she were having trouble understanding my question. "I wouldn't be here if I weren't," she snipped.

I ignored her curt reply. "No, I don't suppose you would. So, in response to your question, in our business, we take advantage of every source we can. These winos are the invisible men around here. Just like maids and butlers, maintenance guys, secretaries, file clerks—those kind of folks. At times, they hear or see things that might point you in the right direction.

"That's the meat and potatoes of this business," I continued as I started down the alley. "Questions, questions, and more questions—of everyone."

"I know that much," she replied tartly. "I spent a year at Texas Investigations."

She was beginning to get on my nerves. "Why'd you leave?"

With a noncommittal shrug, she replied, "I just did."

The south side of the alley behind the torched club was lined with fifty-year-old brick buildings, many deserted, some used as storerooms, and others incidentally used as temporary homes for the transients. I stopped in front of a door directly behind the Hip-Hop and knocked.

No sounds from inside. I knocked again, then pushed the door open.

Over my shoulder, I explained, "This is a storehouse of sorts for the Hip-Hop. Nothing of real value. Some of the winos sleep here from time to time."

The light from the open door illumined the room enough to see it was empty except for a few worn blankets and stained mattresses strewn across the cluttered floor. Sparsely filled shelves lined all four of the brick walls.

Doreen remained outside as I entered and glanced around the main room and the adjoining smaller room.

"Anything in there?"

"Nope. No one," I replied, closing the door behind me.

At that moment, a wizened old man in baggy clothes rounded the corner into the alley. He jerked to a halt when he saw us and immediately turned back in the direction from which he came.

I recognized him immediately. "Hey, Goofyfoot. It's me, Tony, Tony Boudreaux."

He paused and looked around, peering at me skeptically with his watery blue eyes. "Boudreaux?" He took a hesitant step toward us, his baggy coat dragging the ground beside his ragged running shoes.

"Yeah, it's me."

He paused and glanced at Doreen suspiciously. "Who's that?"

"My partner." From the corner of my eyes, I saw her glance at me.

A leering grin split Goofyfoot's wrinkled face, and he cackled. "Business must be good."

"Not bad." I shrugged. I gestured down the alley. "Where's all the boys?"

He shuffled forward, his pigeon-toed foot twisted in

at almost a thirty degree angle. The rubber sole outside his little toe was worn away. He grew serious. "They be around."

I glanced at Doreen. Her lips were curled in disgust. I turned back to Goofyfoot and nodded to the Hip-Hop. "What happened here? I heard they found someone dead out here."

Goofyfoot glanced over his shoulder. "Rosey. It was Rosey."

Rosey! I grimaced. Rosey was one of the first winos I met when I started with Marty. He had provided me with several leads over the years, and in turn I had provided him with the means for several drunks over the years.

Once in the middle of the throes of a three-day drunk, he told me his real name was Chadley Beauregard Collins, and then he swore me to secrecy. "The boys would shame me something terrible," he explained. "They just call me Rosey 'cause after one drink of Thunderbird, my nose turns red."

"Rosey!" I muttered a soft curse. I was going to miss the old man. "What happened?" Goofyfoot hesitated. I grinned and pulled out a twenty. "Here. Now, what happened?"

He drew closer. "Don't rightly know. Me and Downtown was over at the convention center where they had some big dinner and threw away enough to feed us for a year. We was dodging the cops and getting what we could. We heard the sirens and come back. The fire was about out, and there was poor old Rosey lying right there. Blood was leaking from his head." He pointed at the ground where Doreen was standing.

With a sharp gasp, she jumped back.

At last, I told myself, *a human reaction.* "Last I heard, they hadn't identified him. All they know was that he had been struck on the head."

He snorted. "Ain't surprising. Them blueboys, they talk to everybody except them that really knows."

"The cops figure Rosey was the one who burned down the Hip-Hop."

The worn-out old man grunted. "That's stupid. He slept in the back room of the Hip-Hop during cold weather. Why would he burn down his own house?"

"And he slept in the storeroom the rest of the time, huh?"

"Yeah. Rosey, he wasn't much for sleeping outside. He had standards," he added with as much dignity as he could muster.

I glanced at Doreen who, despite the faint curl to her lip, was listening intently. "Tell me, Goofyfoot. You suppose any of the boys know anything about it?"

"Naw." He shook his head. "We talked about it, but no one saw or heard nothing. Shame. Old Rosey, he always shared his goods with us. Sure going to miss that. Why, the week before the fire, he sprung us to a big party right there," he said, nodding to the storeroom.

I laughed. "What happened? He find some rich guy's billfold?"

"Not that. No, sir." He paused and frowned. "I don't rightly know what it was he found, but whatever it was, he pawned it. Got fifty bucks for it."

Doreen and I looked at each other, puzzled. I turned back to Goofyfoot. "He didn't say what it was, huh?"

"Nope." He paused to pull out a battered pack of Pall Mall cigarettes. His nicotine-stained fingers shook as he touched a match to one. "He said he got fifty bucks for it and waved the claim ticket in front of us. And then he bragged someone might give him another fifty for the pawn ticket."

Now, I was curious. What could a wino like Rosey pawn for $50.00? And who would pay him for the ticket? "That's all he said about it?"

With a shrug, Goofyfoot added, "Said he found it in the alley behind the Blackhawk Towers on Congress Avenue on—" He grimaced. "I—I don't remember exactly when, but two or three days before the Hip-Hop burned."

Doreen glanced up at me. "Do you think that had something to do with the fire?"

"Beats me," I replied. "Probably not, but something's odd here."

"What do you mean?"

I studied her a moment, trying to sort my thoughts.

At that moment, a black-and-white cruiser turned into the alley from the far end of the block. Goofyfoot vanished around the corner. Doreen and I stepped out of the way, but the cruiser braked to a halt and the officer eyed us suspiciously.

"What's going on here?" His eyes narrowed. "If this is what I think it is sister, you better move your fanny. We don't allow no soliciting in this town."

Doreen's eyes grew wide and a crimson blush rose in her cheeks.

Hastily I replied, "Not a thing, officer. My partner and I are with the insurance company covering this building. We're investigating the owner's claim, that's all."

He considered my answer, then nodded. "Well, just watch out for yourselves." He eyed Doreen a moment, then added, "Sorry, Ma'am, but this section of town's thick with hookers. Some of them are dressed as fancy as you. You never would guess they were hustling. They look more like they was going to a PTA meeting."

After the black-and-white disappeared around the corner, Doreen sputtered, "I have never been so humiliated in my life. Why, I—"

"Calm down, calm down," I interrupted. "This sort of thing is typical for the business."

At that moment, Buck Topper came out the back door of the Red Rabbit and spotted us. "Hey, Tony. Getdown just called. He'll be here about an hour."

I waved and glanced at my watch. "That gives us time to do a little leg work. Let's go."

Chapter Four

Though I didn't particularly care for Doreen's curt manner, I had to admit she was as cooperative as a puppy chasing a stick. She caught up with me. "Where are we going?"

"Morgue, then the Blackhawk Towers."

I paused at my pickup. "You want to ride or follow." I nodded to her Jag. "You got a good parking spot there, and old Buck is watching the car. You might not get so lucky when we get back."

Pursing her lips, Doreen eyed my pickup, then blew noisily out through them. "I swore I'd never ride in one of these things again, but—well, okay." After she slammed the door behind her and buckled her seatbelt, she looked over at me. "What are you going to do if there's no parking spots when we get back?"

With a chuckle, I pulled away from the curb. "I got a secret."

"What?"

"You'll see." I hesitated, then asked, "Why don't you like to ride in pickups?"

For a moment, she didn't answer. Then she replied vaguely. "I just don't. So, what's at the morgue?"

"You ever been to one?"

She hesitated, then shook her head. "No."

I could see the trepidation in her eyes. I gave her a crooked grin. "Don't worry. We aren't going to see any stiffs. I'm curious about that claim ticket."

"I don't understand."

I flexed my fingers about the wheel. "Stop and think at what we learned. Rosey finds something. He sells it. Then the place where he sleeps burns, and he's hit on the head." I tried to sort and catalog my thoughts. "Like Goofyfoot said, Rosey's not going to burn his house, so if we discount the idea that he did, then what we have left are a couple little theories."

"Such as?"

"First, he stumbled on the arsonist and was killed to keep from identifying him. Second, what if for some reason, someone took whatever it was that Rosey had—maybe the pawn ticket—and killed him. Then the unknown killer burned the bar thinking Rosey would go up with it. But the old man managed to crawl out of the building. And then third, what if for some reason, the killer didn't get what he was looking for?"

Doreen arched an eyebrow. "Sounds like to me you're just guessing."

With a chuckle, I grinned at her. "I am, big time. But, we got to have us a starting place. Besides, we've got an hour to kill before Getdown Joe shows up."

Doreen pulled out a small pad and scribbled some notes.

I frowned. "What's that?"

With the same dour expression on her face, she replied, "I'm making notes."

Despite my mixed feelings toward her, I muttered, "I'm glad to see that."

She looked up, a puzzled frown replacing the sour expression on her face.

I pulled up to a red light and opened my cell phone. I called Billy Joe Martin at the morgue. He and I went back years at Sam Houston University in Huntsville.

I explained I knew the identity of the old wino they had autopsied last week, and that I was looking for a pawn ticket in his effects.

"Come on over, Tony. I'll see what I can find out."

I dropped the cell phone in my pocket.

"Friend of yours?" Her tone didn't have as sharp an edge as earlier.

"Yeah. We were in the Criminal Justice program up at Huntsville until I changed majors."

She arched a curious eyebrow.

I chuckled. "I decided to teach English."

Her eyes grew wide.

"Hey," I added with a grin. "It takes all kinds."

"An English teacher, huh?"

I couldn't be sure, but I thought I caught a fleeting smile over her lips. "Yeah." I sighed and flexed my fingers about the steering wheel. "English in a school where kids didn't want to learn and where every administrator's mission in life was to please the parents."

For a moment, I figured that maybe we were beginning to communicate. "What about you? How'd you end up here?"

Her face grew hard, and the tone in her voice indicated she didn't want to talk about it. "Let's just say it was a choice I made."

I glanced at Doreen as we pushed through the glass doors at the Travis County Morgue. Against the far wall was a semicircular counter behind which sat three mature women in front of computers. I nodded to the first and smiled. "Could you tell Billy Joe Martin that Tony Boudreaux is here?"

She reached for the phone and indicated a row of leather chairs against one wall. "You can wait over there."

As we waited, Doreen scribbled a few additional notes in her notepad. After she dropped it back in her pocket, she looked around at me. "From what you said earlier, I assume you take notes also, huh?"

I nodded. "Yeah." I pulled out several blank 3×5 cards from my pocket. "This is what I keep my notes on. Each card details a single factor: a comment, an act, anything pertaining to the case. Detailed note taking is essential. You're smart to do it."

To my surprise, she smiled. "Thanks."

"Hey, Tony."

We looked around as Billy Joe pushed through the door and let it swing shut behind him. I jumped to my feet, my eyes fixed on his hands, which held nothing. A wave of disappointment washed over me.

He hurried over, and we shook hands. I introduced him to Doreen. "Sorry, Tony. All the old man had on him was thirty-six cents in change and a bag of Bull Durham tobacco."

"And that's it?"

"That's it. By the way, you said you had his name."

Disappointed, I nodded. "Yeah. Chadley Beauregard Collins, nickname, Rosey."

Billy Joe whistled. "Hey, I think if that was my name, I'd go by Rosey too. You know where he came from?"

"No. I met him on Sixth Street a few years ago. You finished with him?"

"Yeah. We'll plant him tomorrow."

I glanced at Doreen, then leaned toward Billy Joe. "I want to give this old man something better than Potter's Field. I'll make arrangements with Maxton Funeral Home to pick him up."

A perplexed frown played over Billy Joe's face and then an expression of understanding replaced it. He winked at me. "If you need a few extra bucks, let me know."

"Thanks, buddy."

Back in the pickup, Doreen looked at me curiously and then buckled herself in. Her eyes fixed on the road ahead, she said, "What was that all about, the funeral home business?"

With a shrug, I brushed her question off. "Nothing."

She eyed me a few moments, then asked, "Did we find out anything important back there?"

Pulling out of the parking lot, I headed back to the Red Rabbit on Sixth Street. "Sometimes, it isn't what we find, but what we don't find."

Her brows knit. "You lost me."

"Remember my little theories. One of them was that perhaps the killer had not found the pawn ticket?" She nodded, and I continued. "But since it wasn't in Rosey's effects, then I think we can say the killer did get it. Follow me?"

A confused expression knit her brows.

I explained, "All that means is we've got one less theory to research."

She shook her head slowly. "That isn't much."

A chuckle rolled off my lips. "No, but it's more than we had a hour ago."

We rode in silence for several moments. Finally, she cleared her throat. "I get the feeling you don't want to talk about it, but that was a nice thing you did back there."

I looked around at her. "What?"

"Burying the old man."

I didn't know her well enough to explain about my own father, and how, if sometime, somewhere, he were found dead in an alleyway in Dallas or the park in Tucson, someone would give him a decent burial. I flexed my fingers about the steering wheel. "Thanks."

At that moment, we pulled up in front of the Red Rabbit. There were no parking spots. Doreen looked around at me with a smug grin on her face. "No parking spots, so what's your secret?"

I whipped into a loading zone behind her red Jag and hopped out.

"You're begging for a ticket."

"Think so?" I grinned at her and tilted the back of the seat forward. I rummaged through a dozen magnetized signs until I found the one I wanted. I pulled it out and slammed the door. "Here's the secret," I said with a smug grin of my own.

The sign read, *Blevin's Brewery: We Deliver.* And I promptly stuck it on the side of the door.

Doreen arched an eyebrow. "Who's going to believe that?"

I laughed. "Everyone."

Chapter Five

As we entered the open door of the bar, I spotted Getdown in the rear of the room. Seated across the table from him was a light-complexioned black man with a shiny bald head.

At that moment, a cockroach the size of a rat scurried across the worn wooden floor in front of us. Doreen stiffened. "Ugh."

I chuckled. "Steady there," I quipped. "I'll defend you."

She didn't laugh. I rolled my eyes.

At seventy-four, Getdown Joe Sillery had successfully managed to stay aboard the roller coaster ride of a business that teetered precariously on the brink between the law and the lawless. Rumor had it Getdown had solid mob connections. Rumor had it he was big time into drugs. Rumor also had it that if you sent a particular e-mail to five hundred people, Dell Computers would give you a laptop.

I shouldn't admit it, but I know for a fact they do not.

That's why I never paid any attention to rumors.

The fat man was cleaning up a platter that, if it were his usual brunch, had once held four cheeseburgers, fries, and two apple turnovers. As we drew near, the light-complexioned young man rose and disappeared down the hall to the rear of the building.

Getdown Joe barely topped five feet, both in height and width. He rolled when he walked, but he was rightly labeled as the biggest proponent of Hip-Hop in Austin. His club was routinely jammed with customers, all more than willing to pay the exorbitant prices his club demanded.

Licking the grease from his sausage-thick fingers, he looked up at us. "You the ones Blevins' sent?'

"Yeah." I introduced Doreen and myself. "We've been doing a little snooping around." The leftover aromas of the greasy cheeseburgers floating above the table were mouth watering. Behind me, I heard Doreen's stomach growl.

He gestured to the chairs at the table. He shook his head. "Don't it figure. Take off a couple days and things always go down the tubes." He nodded down the hall into which the younger man had disappeared. "Even them that work for you don't care just as long as they get their bread every week."

"You've been gone, huh? Vacation?" I asked casually as I slipped in at the table.

"In a way. I wanted to catch a new rap group up in Dallas at the Somalia Sunrise Club."

Buck stopped at the table. "You want anything?"

Before I could reply, Doreen answered. "No. Nothing."

Unlike many who attempt to hide their girth with garish clothes, Getdown's dress was much more fashionable than mine. Of course, just about any mode of dress is more fashionable than washed-out jeans, running shoes, and a sports coat over a Polo shirt. He grunted. "Fawn had some good things to say about you, Boudreaux."

Of that I wasn't surprised. Fawn Williams was a high-class escort out of Lafayette whom I managed to clear of a murder earlier that year. "Good. Now, about the fire. The cops figured Rosey was the one who set it."

His rotund face froze. He stared at me in disbelief, the white of his eyes accenting the surprise in his pupils. "Rosey? Was that who that old man was? The cops said they couldn't identify him."

"That's who it was. Goofyfoot told us."

He muttered a soft curse. "He was a harmless old bum. Sometimes in the winter, he slept in the back room of my club." He paused. "So, what do you think?"

I gave Doreen a warning look. "I think whoever torched your place didn't want Rosey to identify him, so he killed the old man."

Getdown Joe gulped a swallow of beer from an icy mug and waved to Buck for a refill. "So you think someone else torched it, huh?"

"Yeah."

He grunted. "That's what I think too."

"I haven't talked to the insurance company, but from the looks of your place, it was a total loss."

"Yeah. And I had a backroom full of beer and wine plus all of my cloth goods."

"Cloth goods?"

"Yeah, you know. Towels for the bar and restrooms, tablecloths, and new uniforms for my people."

"Uniforms?"

A wide grin split his face, his brilliantly white teeth a striking contrast to his blue-black skin. "Yeah. The laundry had a supply of uniforms they got stuck with when the Elegante Club shut down. I ain't seen them, but I figured they would give the Hip-Hop a little more class."

For a fleeting moment, a random thought nagged at me, but I couldn't quite pull it out. I continued. "My boss said you had an idea someone was trying to teach you a lesson."

"Yeah." He grunted. "In the last two months, I got me four offers on the place." He paused as Buck slid the beer on the table. After Buck left, he continued. "And I wasn't even hustling the place. It's a money maker." He laughed. "It's like printing my own money."

I pulled out a note card. "Who were they?"

He cut his eyes to Doreen, then back to me. "Patsy Fusco from San Antonio, Mossy Eisen from Atlanta, and someone named Abe Romero. I never heard of him. That's it."

Pausing with the tip of my pen to the note card, I looked up at him. "You said four."

"Fusco sent two proposals. He's always been a pushy brother."

"Any others? What about around here on the street? Anyone want your club?"

"Are you kidding? Half of them would slit the other half's throats for it. Like I said, it's better than a printing press."

"What about Calvin?"

Getdown frowned. "Next door at the Bistro?"

"Yeah."

"No. He has his own little enterprises."

I wanted to ask if Calvin's little enterprises involved drugs, but I know what Getdown's answer would be. I hooked my thumb over my shoulder. "What about Buck?"

Lifting an eyebrow, Getdown grinned. "He wants to expand."

"Enough to torch your place?"

The rotund man shook his head. "He ain't smart enough to do it without getting caught, but he is just smart enough realize that."

"What does your insurance company say?"

He shrugged. "You know those guys. Now, they claim I was over–insured. They sure wasn't saying that when they took them premiums I paid each month, those bunch of blood-sucking—" He paused and glanced at Doreen. "Jerks." He paused. "So, you going to be able to help me?"

I grinned at him. "I've tracked down alligators in the Louisiana swamp. I can find something as simple as a torch man."

He laughed loudly. "I hopes so. I'm ready to rebuild that sucker, and I sure don't want some Bright Skin burning it down again."

I looked up at him in surprise. "Bright Skin? Are you sure? How do you know it was a white man?"

His pie-shaped face contorted in a frown. "I don't rightly, but a couple days after the place burned down, I spotted a Bright Skin leaving my storeroom in the alley."

"Could it have been one of the transients? I heard Rosey and some others slept out there during the warm months."

"None of them winos could afford the set of drapes that dude was wearing."

Suppressing the surge of excitement boiling through my veins, I studied him a moment. *And maybe*, I told myself, *whoever killed Rosey didn't find the pawn ticket after all.*

Back on the sidewalk, Doreen turned to me. "I'm hungry. Is there someplace to eat around here?"

Remembering her reaction to the cockroach, I kept a straight face. "You should have ordered something back there. The cheeseburgers smelled out of this world."

She curled her lips. "In that dump? Not on your life."

I chuckled and nodded at Fat Sal's Bistro next to the Lighthouse across the street. "They have a fair deli over there. "And," I added before she had a chance to reply, "no roaches."

I ordered a small bowl of chicken potpie, and Doreen opted for chicken gumbo. While we waited for our lunch, I pulled out my ubiquitous 3×5 note cards and began jotting down more information from the interview with Getdown.

Doreen frowned. "Why do you use note cards? Why not a notebook like I have?"

I explained. "One idea, one card. That way I can juggle them around. You know, sort of rearrange my ideas." With a shrug, I added, "Sometimes it helps see the problem from a different angle."

When the solemn waitress delivered our lunch, I eyed Doreen's watery gumbo skeptically. "One of these days, I'll whip up a real gumbo for you. Let you see what the original tastes like."

Dabbing her lips daintily with a napkin, she arched an eyebrow. "You're from Louisiana, huh?"

"Yeah. How'd you know?"

"The business about the alligator and now the gumbo."

"Hey, you might make a fair detective yet."

That time, she almost smiled.

After lunch, I headed back to the storeroom, explaining I wanted to take another look at it. Though puzzled, Doreen stayed at my side. "So," she asked as I pushed open the door, "what do you expect to find in there? You looked at it this morning."

With my hand on the knob, I turned to face her. "Remember what Getdown Joe said about seeing a well-dressed dude leave the place?" She nodded, and I continued. "What's someone all duded up doing back here? This isn't exactly the kind of place someone like that would spend time browsing. He was looking for something." I opened the door. A musty odor filled the room.

Her eyes grew wide. "The pawn ticket?"

"Why not?" I shrugged, flipping on the light switch. The switch plate rattled, but I thought nothing of it. Below the switch, a water faucet extended a few inches from the brick wall.

She looked around the storeroom. "Not much here."

She was right. Covered by dust, a dozen boxes or so were stacked on the shelves lining the walls of the room. Wrinkled blankets and stained mattresses were jammed under the shelves. In the middle of the floor was an empty wooden crate with a clutter of cardboard boxes surrounding it. On the fourth wall, a door to the smaller room separated the shelves. Doreen pointed to it. "What's in there?"

"Another storeroom."

"So, what now?"

"Let's take it methodically. We'll begin in here. You start with that wall; I'll start with this one. We'll meet on the far side. Then, we'll do the other room."

"What about the boxes on the shelves?"

"Them too. And look for any nooks and crannies where a pawn ticket could be hidden."

For the next thirty minutes, we searched on top of the shelves, under the shelves, and behind the shelves. We opened boxes filled with everything from St. Patrick's Day napkins to jars of rancid olives.

We checked the stained and dirty mattresses for cuts into which the ticket could have been hidden. I suppressed a chuckle when Doreen daintily tried to handle the soiled mattresses with just her forefinger and thumb. In one corner, we found an empty gallon fuel container. I sniffed it. Empty now, it had once contained gasoline.

By now, we were both dirty and sweaty despite the cool day.

I nodded to the closed door. "Nothing out here. Let's try that room."

I pushed open the door and stepped inside.

A heavy blow slammed into my back. My head snapped back and the force propelled me across the small room and into the wall. My head bounced off the brick. My legs grew weak, and just before I sagged to the floor, I heard Doreen scream.

Chapter Six

Doreen's scream cut through the wooziness in my head. I managed to push myself to my feet and stagger to the door. I tried to focus my eyes, and then I felt something warn running down either side of the bridge of my nose. I wiped at it and pulled away a hand smeared with blood.

"Tony! Help me out of here!" Doreen's voice was strident, demanding.

Pulling out my handkerchief, I dabbed at the blood coming from the split in my forehead. When I finally focused my eyes, I saw Doreen, bent double, her derrière stuck in the wooden box, her feet almost even with her head.

She screamed again. "Get me out of here!"

The blow to the head had addled me. I staggered

uncertainly across the room and, holding the handkerchief to my bleeding forehead with one hand, I grabbed one of her flailing arms and managed to pull her from the box.

She was livid with anger. "If I get my hands on that—" She muttered a few descriptive epithets I was surprised she knew.

She had been too angry to notice I was bleeding. When she did, the anger fled her face, and she hurried to me. "You hurt yourself!" She said it as if it were my fault.

My throbbing head plus her unfriendly manner all day got the best of me. "Brilliant observation, Detective," I muttered, shaking my head in frustration and wobbling over to the water faucet by the front door. I splashed water over my face and dried it with the handkerchief.

Doreen stood at my side, silently looking on. I don't know what I expected. Perhaps a couple words of sympathy or concern, but after a few moments, I decided that maybe she was one of those who thought sympathy or concern was a weakness. Or maybe she just didn't care. Still bent over, I closed my eyes and mumbled. "Jeez, what a day."

Finally, I straightened and drew a deep breath. "Did you get a good look at the guy?"

"Not really. He was big—taller than you—and dressed very well in a blue suit, with pinstripes." She frowned. "His nose looked funny, and he had a ponytail."

My eyes started to lose focus. I put out my hand to the wall to steady myself. "His nose? Funny? Like what?"

"I don't know. Sort of, well, flat."

"Like a boxer's?"

She shrugged. "I don't know. I never watch boxing."

Holding the handkerchief to my forehead, I headed unsteadily back to my pickup. "Tell you what. I've got one more stop, but why don't you head on back to the office. Use my computer and write up a report of what we did this morning. I've got about an hour's worth of running around to do. When I come in, we'll get together and see just where we stand."

She nodded and brushed at the dirt on her clothes. "If you say so." She looked around the alley distastefully. "I'll be more than happy to get out of here."

All I could do was nod slowly. I was more than happy for her to get out of here. I've always been one of those who try to find excuses for others' behavior—and for the most part, I've been able to work with just about anyone—but right now, my head was hurting, I was bleeding, my clothes were dirty, and I wasn't in the mood to put up with a recalcitrant child any longer.

To be honest, the report was something to keep her out of my hair for the rest of the afternoon.

And when I got back to the office, Marty Blevins was going to get a piece of my mind. No one deserves to be saddled with someone brandishing an attitude that would make Attila the Hun look like a choirboy.

After she drove away, I went into the Red Rabbit and washed up in the men's room in an effort to make myself halfway presentable. After bumming a Band-Aid from Buck and combing my hair, I headed for the Blackhawk Towers.

The Blackhawk Towers was busy with at least three different conventions checking in, one them being the State Patrolman's Association. While waiting at the reception desk as three busy clerks helped patrons check in, I spotted the placard on a easel welcoming the association to Austin was signed by the Chief of Police, Ramon Pachuca.

Over the last few years, I'd turned to Ramon for help in a few instances, and as long as I didn't stick my nose into police business, he was always accommodating. I wouldn't go as far as to say we were drinking buddies, but on several occasions, he'd helped me out of a bind.

At that moment, a clerk spoke up. "Yes, sir. How can I help you?" She glanced at the Band-Aid on my forehead.

"I'd like to see the manager, please."

She hesitated. "May I ask the purpose of your business, please?"

I did what I do a lot. I lied. Gesturing to the placard, I said, "I was talking to Chief Pachuca." I paused for effect, then added, "The Chief of Police of the Austin Police Department. You know him?" Before she could answer, I continued, "Anyway, he suggested I visit with the hotel manager about a situation, one which I am not at liberty to discuss with anyone except your manager, miss."

She stared at me a moment, then quickly disappeared through a door behind the counter. Moments later, an obviously puzzled manager hurried out, his gaze darting about the lobby at the collection of police uniforms.

"Yes, sir. There's no trouble is there, sir?" His gaze kept shifting back to the uniforms gathering on the far side of the lobby.

"No." I identified myself and explained I was investigating a case. "I need to learn if a week or so back, around the fifteenth, any of your guests reported any valuables missing."

He frowned. "I—ah, I'm afraid I don't understand."

Patiently, I explained. "An item was found in one of your dumpsters and pawned. We don't know what it was, but there's reason to believe it has value. What I'm trying to find out is if any of your guests reported any valuables missing around the fourteenth or fifteenth. That's all."

He pursed his lips and rubbed his hands nervously. He stammered, "I—I'm not sure I can provide—ah—ah—that information without going through the proper channels."

I glanced at his nametag. "Look, Mister Lane. I can get a warrant, or—" I pointed to the gathering of uniforms across the lobby. "Or I can go over there and find Ramon Pachuca, police chief of Austin PD. You might listen to him, but you know, that's a lot of trouble for everyone."

He hesitated.

I noticed one of the uniforms looking in my direction. I waved. He had no idea who I was, but he waved back. "That's Ramon," I said with a straight face.

The manager blurted out. "That won't be necessary. Please come with me. All thefts are reported to House-keeping, which then sends me copies of the reports. I have them in my office."

In his office, he led the way to a bank of file cabinets, and slid out a drawer. "Here, Mister Boudreaux. I don't remember if there were any reports or not, but you can see for yourself. They're filed by date."

To my surprise, there were very few theft reports, and nothing for two or three days on either side of the sixteenth and seventeenth.

I closed the drawer and turned to the manager. "See how simple that was. I appreciate your cooperation."

His smile became condescending. "We always try to help the law, Mister Boudreaux."

Back in my pickup, I tried to rethink what I had learned. Rosey had found something. Whatever it was, it had value, obviously much more than the fifty bucks Goofyfoot claimed. Pawn brokers are not known for their generosity and warm fuzzies. If they loaned fifty bucks on an item, it had to be worth several times that much.

Whatever the value, it was enough to get Rosey killed. So if it were that valuable, why wasn't the theft reported?

Unless—I nodded. Why didn't I think of that before?

One reason some missing valuables are not reported is the same reason a drug lord wouldn't report a missing suitcase of money. The items were stolen or illegal.

On impulse, I climbed out of my pickup and walked down the recently washed-down alley where the Blackhawk Towers kept its Dumpsters. I stood there studying the four of them lined up along the rear wall of the hotel.

Suppose whoever lost the item had never been at the Blackhawk? Suppose he was just looking for a place to dump it so he could later retrieve it?

Then Rosey stumbled onto it.

I looked up and down the alley. All a person driving past had to do was open the window and toss the item into the Dumpster. But, if that were the case, how would he know Rosey was the one who found the item? The old wino seldom ventured more than half-a-dozen blocks from Sixth Street. That meant whoever killed Rosey might possibly be a street regular who picked up word of Rosey's windfall from someone on the street.

Scratching my jaw, I tried to remember some of Rosey's back-alley cohorts. Goofyfoot and Downtown came to mind instantly. Try as I could, I couldn't recollect the others.

Avoiding puddles of water and staying next to the hotel wall so I would be out of any alley traffic, I headed back to my pickup, still pondering my newest theory that the killer was from Sixth Street.

Suddenly, the squeal of tires jerked me back to the present. At the end of the alley, the bigger-than-life grill of a massive Lincoln Town Car snarled at me as the heavy car scraped along the hotel wall, sparks flying as it bore down on me. The engine erupted from a roar to a howling scream, and the massive vehicle leaped forward.

I glimpsed a face covered by a ski mask behind the wheel just as I spun and raced for the Dumpsters thirty feet away. I dared not glance over my shoulder. I could hear the tires splashing through the puddles of water. I ran harder. My heart pounded against my chest.

Clenching my teeth, I kept my eyes on the ten-foot space between the first two Dumpsters. That was my closest sanctuary.

The last five or six steps, I expected the impact of the massive grill. I leaped into the gap, landing on my shoulder and rolling over, but I didn't have time to relax.

Tires bit into the alley, squealing on the dry spots as the Lincoln shot backward. The engine roared again, followed by the deafening clangor of metal as the Lincoln slammed into the Dumpster, knocking it several feet toward me. I leaped back, bouncing off the second Dumpster, and then came the high-pitched shriek of metal against metal as the first Dumpster started moving inexorably toward me again. Without hesitation, I darted from my would-be sanctuary and dashed down the alley.

I've always been kind to animals, so that, and not my dashing good looks or charming manner, must have been why the good Lord at that moment sent a delivery truck into the alley from the opposite end of the block.

As I raced past the delivery truck, I remembered the other winos who hung with Goofyfoot and Downtown—Spryo and Pookie.

Chapter Seven

I had no idea what I had stumbled into, but by the time I jumped in my pickup and pulled back into the traffic, I knew that obviously, someone did not want anyone nosing into the affair I had blundered upon. And they were serious enough not to stop with a single murder. I glanced at my coat and muttered a curse. When I landed on my shoulder between the Dumpsters, I'd ripped a shoulder seam.

As soon as I parked outside our office, I called Danny O'Banion. A polite description of him is a local entrepreneur with his fingers and toes in every pot in Travis County. Actually, he's Austin's resident mobster. Of course, no one calls him that to his face, but the best I can figure is he's about half a step below the family concierge. Perhaps, a better explanation is that he's the concierge for the concierges, a sort of liaison between those at the top and the soldiers at the bottom.

I set up a meeting with him for 6:00 that afternoon.

After punching off, I called Jerry Blue at Texas Investigations. We'd known each other for five years, and when I asked about Doreen Patterson, he groaned. "I'm glad you got her instead of us. She was a pain in the neck."

"How so?"

"She likes to work by herself. Only trouble is, she don't want to dig too deep. You know, go the limit to top off a case. And she don't care for men. We ended up having her do skips and traces."

"What happened? Why'd she leave?"

"She didn't. I let her go. Too stinking hard to work with."

When I walked into the office, I spotted Doreen at my desk, using my computer. When she saw me, she nodded to the computer monitor. "Here's your report," she said woodenly. "I didn't know what format you preferred, so I did the best I could. I gave Marty a copy. We can make any changes you want."

Bending over her shoulder, I read the day's report on the monitor. While she was thorough, she showed little perception. It was a bland report, holding no theories up for inspection. *The product,* I told myself, *of someone who was super-organized and worked strictly out of the left side of the brain, refusing to recognize questions raised by the right side.*

"Did you find anything else after I left?" She eyed the ripped seam on my jacket.

Before I could answer, Marty came out of his office with a copy of her report. He waddled over to my desk.

His cheeks were rosy and the veins in his bulbous nose stood out. He'd been hitting the vodka, which was no surprise. He hit it everyday. He waved the report and in an effort to be humorous, said, "Looks like you two had a good time today. You manage to get any work in?"

In all honesty, I knew he was trying in his inimitable way to be funny, but I was already ticked off at him, and the tone in his voice pushed me over the edge. "Not by a long sight, Marty," I snapped. I jabbed a finger in the ripped seam on my shoulder. "It just so happened that someone tried to make me a hood ornament for a Lincoln, someone connected with the fire. Is that enough work for you or do you want more? Maybe a busted leg or a broken arm?"

My tirade set him back on his heels. "Hold on, Tony, hold on. All I meant was—" He held out the report. "I mean, after I read this, I—"

"You weren't supposed to read it until I got back, and we put the whole thing together."

"Okay, okay." His tone grew patronizing. "So, where do we stand?"

For the next twenty minutes, I explained all that had happened, making it a point to stress the questions raised by various events throughout the day.

"So, the way I see it right now," I added, "whoever killed Rosey torched the club as a cover up."

"Any ideas?"

I pointed to the report in his hand. "The names on there: Patsy Fusco, Mossy Eisen, and some guy named Abe Romero. And maybe a couple more on the street. I'll know more the next couple days."

Marty knit his brows. "Understand, Tony. I'm more concerned about nailing the joker who torched the place than I am an old wino's killer."

Suppressing the burst of anger coursing through my veins, I replied in a strained voice, "I'll find the torch man, Marty, but I am going to find Rosey's killer. I owe the old man that much."

For several moments, we stared at each other until he shrugged. "As long as we get the torch man."

"We will. I've got a meeting with Danny O'Banion this evening. He ought to be able to give me some help with those three names."

Doreen frowned. "O'Banion? The mobster? How can he help?"

For several moments I studied her, puzzling over how little she seemed to be aware of the mechanics of our business. Even with only a year's experience, she should have been more cognizant of the sundry sources of information on which our line of work had to draw.

"He can," was my only reply.

She shrugged. "What time do we see him?"

While Danny would have welcomed any of my friends, I'd had my fill of Ms. Doreen Patterson for the day, so I glibly lied. "Just me. Danny doesn't like newcomers."

She glanced hopefully at Marty. He grinned sheepishly at her. "Why don't you give it a try, Tony? After all, the more people she meets, the better it will be for her, and the better it is for her, the better off our company is."

I shook my head and told another lie. "I'm not going to put any pressure on Danny, Marty. He's helped us out of more than one bad spot. You've always let me handle Danny. Don't change anything now."

He ran his thick fingers over his sweaty forehead uncomfortably. "Look, you and O'Banion go back to high school together. Won't that mean something to him?"

"It might, but I don't want to take a chance." I looked at Doreen. "Sorry, but this is one relationship I don't want to jeopardize." I felt guilty about lying to her, but not enough to take her with me. I pointed to my ripped jacket. "I'm going to put on a change of clothes before I see him." I started for the door. "I'll see you two tomorrow."

Marty called out. "Wait up, Tony. I'll walk you to the elevator. I have another case to talk to you about."

"Huh?" I turned to face him. Marty never walked anybody anywhere. He was up to something.

He winked and repeated. "I'll walk you to the elevator."

When the office door closed behind us, Marty began to plead. "Look, Tony. I'm in a bind. Doreen in there is my wife's little sister. She's been divorced for five years, bounced around through a half-dozen relationships. Thank the Lord, there weren't no kids. She don't like them. Anyway, last week, she got canned over at Texas Investigations, and Dora hounded me until I hired her."

I glared at him. "Why didn't you tell me this right off the bat? I was miserable out there today with her. At least, I would have known what was going on. She's no help, just trouble. I'd rather put up with a dozen Louisiana alligators. That's why I sent her back to do that fake report. Just to get her out of my hair."

He chuckled. "I wondered what prompted you to do one. Anyway, I'm sorry, but I figured you being pretty much laid back and an ex-schoolteacher, you could put up with her easier than the other guys. I'm afraid Al would punch her out, that temper of his. Besides, I don't look for her to stay. I figure after a couple weeks, she'll bail out. If she does it on her own, then Dora can't get on my back. You know what I mean?"

I knew exactly what he meant. While I had never met his wife socially, I had, on more than one occasion, witnessed her storming in and literally kicking off World War III in Marty's office. The USS Blevins was the unbecoming nickname pasted on her by the guys in the office.

"I don't know, Marty."

"Come on, Tony. Next time you need a favor, all you got to do is ask. I really need some help here."

My determination began to crumble. "How many weeks?"

"Two. I promise. Two."

I figured I would regret helping him. "No more than two. If she's still here, you promise you'll put her with someone else. Right?"

He gave me a hearty slap on the shoulder. "A promise in blood, Tony. I swear."

"You don't have blood, Marty. You have vodka."

He grinned. "Okay, in vodka."

I had the feeling I just taken my first step into a watery bed of quicksand. "All right. Have her meet me out in the parking lot at five-thirty."

On the way to my apartment on Payton Gin Road, I remembered Marty's remark about expecting Doreen to bail out of the job. Now, I wouldn't be honest if I didn't admit considering various means to encourage her to move on, but I knew if I did something underhanded, my Catholic conscience and my mother's face would nag at me forever. And that would be more uncomfortable than tolerating Doreen for the next two weeks. Nope, I was better off just doing my job and leting nature take its course.

Besides, who could say? Many of us fail over and over until finally we find our little niche. Because I knew the feeling well, I was always a sucker for those niche-seekers. It wasn't beyond the realm of reason that this might be the niche Doreen was seeking.

Still, I wasn't looking forward to the next two weeks.

Chapter Eight

Before I left my apartment, I called Danny and told him I was bringing my partner.

"No problem," he replied instantly. "The more the merrier."

"This one is a woman," I added.

"That's even better," he gushed. "By the way, are you still seeing that little rich girl? What was her name, Janice?"

I grinned. "Just don't get any ideas. Besides, she's classy, not for the likes of you."

He roared with laughter. "And you think you got class driving around in broken-down pickup. Why, you're just a Louisiana Cajun that slogged out of the swamps and ended up in the great state of Texas, Tony."

I shook my head as I replaced the receiver. Danny

was a good friend, and I had never tried to reconcile the fact he was on one side of the law, and I was on the other. That was one little detail we simply ignored.

Doreen was sitting in her Jag in the parking lot when I pulled in. I stopped beside her and rolled down the window. "Hop in."

She shook her head. "I'll follow you."

I'd made up my mind not to tap dance around the situation. All day, I'd been uncomfortable around her. Of course, I had to admit it was by my choice, deferring to her insistence of being formally addressed, following me in her car, and her obvious repugnance toward Goofyfoot. Maybe I was wrong, but I sensed she felt she was superior to those about her. I had no intention of enduring another two weeks like that.

I decided to run the flag up the pole, express my feelings, and see which way the wind blew the flag. "Nope. If you go, it's in my pickup. Besides, we need to talk."

She frowned. "About what?"

"You'll see. Are you going?"

She studied me for several seconds, then with a disgusted shake of her head, climbed out of the Jag.

Buckling her seat belt, she demanded, "All right. What is it you want to talk about?"

I've never traveled the world, but I can't believe any city in any country has worse traffic at 5:30 in the afternoon than Austin, Texas. Interstate lanes packed with side-by-side, bumper-to-bumper traffic stretch for miles, and you've got to feel sorry for the poor slob who tries to enter from an on-ramp, which is probably also backed up for miles.

Streets for a mile on either side of the Interstate catch the overflow traffic. The gridlock is so complex that one simple fender-bender could hold up traffic for hours.

So, when we pulled out into the traffic heading for downtown, I kept my eyes on the road. "I want to talk about you and me, Doreen."

She jerked around and gave me a blistering look when I used her given name.

I continued, not planning on saying anything that would create any more dissension between Marty and the USS Bl—oops, I mean, Marty and his wife. "Marty told me about your situation, that you'd left Texas Investigation and that you were his sister-in-law. He also mentioned you were divorced a few years ago. Now, in this business, we have to work together. From now on, I'm Tony and you're Doreen. We don't have to like each other, although that would make things much more comfortable, but we do have to cooperate with each other—sort of use each other for a sounding board."

I paused, expecting a heated retort. When she remained silent, I continued. "I contacted a friend at Texas Investigation. You didn't leave; they fired you. He said you were hard to work with." I glanced at her from the corner of my eye. She was staring straight ahead and her fists were clenched in her lap. I continued. "Now, I don't know about any of that. I don't care about any of that.

All I know is that you could find a home here at Blevins'. If you want my help, I'll be more than happy to do whatever I can. And yeah, sometimes we work with the dregs of society. That's just the way it is." I chuckled. "But the truth is, Blevins' isn't really such a bad place, and the job isn't a bad job."

For several moments, the only sound was the clamor of traffic. I didn't know if I'd been too abrupt or too subtle. Finally, she cleared her throat. "My brother-in-law talks too much."

I laughed. "I won't argue that."

"Did he tell you Dora, that's my sister, nagged at him for a week to hire me?"

Honesty is fine, but there is always a time for a little discretion. "Nope."

A few moments later, she asked, "Who did you talk to over at Texas Investigations?"

I arched an eyebrow. "Just a friend." I glanced at her, and for the first time saw a faint smile on her lips.

"And you don't want me to hassle him, huh?"

"Something like that." I had the feeling that perhaps we had broken the proverbial iceberg that seemed to be separating us, but I was mistaken. I might have cracked it, but it wasn't broken. "So, tell me, what happened over there?"

"Nothing I couldn't handle," she replied. Then she changed the subject. "How did you come to know this O'Banion thug?"

I glanced at her sharply.

She saw the anger in my eyes and shrugged. "Well, he is mobster, isn't he?"

Flexing my fingers on the steering wheel, I replied brusquely, "Even if he is, not all mobsters are thugs."

She arched a skeptical eyebrow. "So, how did you two meet? Marty said something about high school."

I drew a deep breath and released it slowly. "Eleventh grade here in Austin. We got into a few schoolboy scrapes together. He dropped out during his senior year, and for a while, we lost touch with each other. Next time I saw him was at the Texas-Oklahoma game up in Dallas. He looked prosperous. We slapped each other on the shoulder, sipped from his flask a little, lied a lot, and then went our separate ways.

"My first year on this job, I saved his bosses a couple suitcases of money, which naturally put me in good with them. Since then, as long as it doesn't affect him, he's given me all the help I've asked for."

"So you think he can help us on this case, huh?"

"I hope so. He knows what's going on in his world. If any of those guys, Fusco, Eisen, or Romero are thinking about moving into the area, he'll know."

"All right. I see what you're getting at. If they're not coming into the area," she said. "That means they'd have no interest in burning down the club, which in turn would eliminate the theory that someone was trying to teach Getdown Joe a lesson."

I grinned at her. "Good thinking. That would support the idea that the club was torched to cover the murder."

She thought for a moment, then remarked, "But still, why would they have even made a contact if they weren't interested?"

I was beginning to like her. "They might have been at the time. But, that, my dear Sherlock, is what we have to find out."

Her eyebrows lifted when we pulled into the Green Light Parking garage. I explained, "Danny's office is on the sixth floor. We'll park down here and take the elevator." I stopped at the gate, and a neatly dressed man in a business suit came out of the small office. "Hello, Tony." He glanced at Doreen and nodded. "Miss." He indicated a slot next to Danny's limo. "You can park over there. Danny's on the way down."

As we pulled into the parking slot, Doreen said, "I've never seen a parking lot boy dressed in a business suit. He was certainly polite."

I chuckled and opened my door. "Just one of your thugs, that's all."

She looked around at me in disbelief. I nodded.

At that moment, the elevator doors hissed open and Huey, aka Godzilla in a gray pinstriped suit, stepped out followed by a grinning Danny O'Banion.

Doreen came to stand by me at the tailgate of the pickup. She gasped at the out-sized bodyguard. "Who— What is that?"

I tilted my head toward her and whispered, "That's Huey, Tony's valet."

She arched a skeptical eyebrow.

Danny waved and called out, "Tony boy. Great to see you."

He grabbed me in a bear hug. "You're looking great." He pulled back and eyed the Band-Aid on my forehead. "Looks like you forgot to duck, huh?"

Before I could respond, he turned to Doreen. "And this is the young woman you told me about." He offered her his hand. "You said she was bright, but you didn't tell me she was also beautiful. I'm Danny O'Banion, Miss—"

With a knowing smile on her lips, Doreen cut her eyes at me, then focused on Danny. "Patterson, Doreen Patterson, Mister O'Banion. And Tony didn't tell me you could put out such beautiful malarkey."

Danny roared. "I love her, Tony. This one is okay." By now, Huey had opened the limo door, and Danny took Doreen by the elbow and ushered her into the rear seat of the limo. "Go around to the other side, Tony," he called over his shoulder. "Or we'll leave you behind."

"Where are we going?" I asked as I slammed the door.

"Where else?"

"County Line?"

"You bet." He scooted around in the seat to face Doreen. "You like barbecue?"

I don't know if Danny noticed it or not, but the look in her eyes didn't match the smile on her lips. "Love it."

"Then you'll like this place. Best barbecue in the state. Isn't that right, Tony? Hand me a beer, Huey. How about it, Doreen? Want one? Bud Lite?"

She eyed the can distastefully. "Perhaps later."

Danny shrugged. "Tony?"

"Not right now. I'll wait for the barbecue."

He chuckled. "Still doing the AA thing, huh?"

"Yeah. Doing okay for the most part." I grinned sheepishly. "Sometimes I fall off the wagon, but I've always figured it was a sin to drink anything but cold beer with good barbecue."

Chapter Nine

Danny kept up a steady stream of chatter all the way to the County Line Barbecue, innocuous chit-chat about her work, his travels, and half-a-dozen inane subjects. Doreen held up her end of the conversation although it seemed to me that most of her responses were a little too succinct, a little too brief. I glanced at Danny from time to time, but he didn't seem to notice, so I just leaned back and relaxed.

I remembered Jerry Blue's comment, "she don't like men." I grinned wryly to myself. This was one heck of a business for a woman who didn't like men.

I made a mental note to query Marty about that remark the next morning.

As usual, County Line was superb. In addition to an

icy pitcher of draft beer, Danny and I ordered the All-You-Can-Eat platter of meaty ribs. With it came a loaf of freshly baked bread and bricks of butter. "What are you going to have?" I asked Doreen.

She shrugged. "I'm not very hungry."

Danny frowned and glanced at me. "I thought you said you loved barbecue, Doreen?"

"I do, but I couldn't handle a full order."

Danny laughed. "Then make it a half order. You'll never forgive yourself if you leave here without their barbecue."

She agreed.

We filled our icy mugs from the pitcher of beer. Doreen sipped hers daintily, then licked the foam from her lips with an experienced touch.

When the ribs arrived, we dug in. I glanced sidelong at Doreen who held the ribs as daintily as she had held the mattresses, but she did a good job cleaning the meat off the bones.

I figured the beer would loosen her up a little, but instead, she became more reserved. She nodded at Huey standing by the door, his massive arms crossed over his barrel chest. "Isn't he going to eat?"

Danny winked at me. "Huey's a vegan. Hates meat."

Doreen frowned at me. I just nodded. She shrugged and poured another mug of beer and attacked another rib.

While we gnawed through rib after rib and downed

beer after beer, we discussed the circumstances surrounding the Hip-Hop.

Danny shrugged. "None of my boys heard a peep about it on the streets. If someone had planned to torch it, they didn't get help from any of the locals."

I touched the Band-Aid over the knot on my forehead. I couldn't help wondering if the goon who had slammed me into the wall earlier that day was a local or someone from outside. I still couldn't shake the feeling that the torching was a cover-up for Rosey's murder.

After licking the thick, sweet sauce from his fingers, Danny nodded and said, "I know Patsy Fusco good, too good. He's ambitious, and he wants to get a toehold in Austin. Eisen, I don't know, but Joe Vasco over in New Orleans probably has a handle on him. I'll get back with you tomorrow. Abe Romero is a small-time staker looking to step up. I can figure him wanting the Hip-Hop, but not even Abe is stupid enough to burn down something he wants."

I glanced at Doreen who was hanging on to every word Danny uttered about the case. "Abe's here in town?"

"Yeah. Last I heard, he hangs out at the Texas Star over in Elgin."

"What about Calvin Engel? He owns Jimmy's Bistro next to the Hip-Hop."

Danny shrugged. "What about him?"

"I heard he was sort of what you would call an entrepreneur. He has his finger in a bunch of pies."

"Small time. Hustles stolen goods from time to time."

"What about drugs?"

"Probably. I never heard, but busters like Engel will stoop to about any level."

Doreen pushed back from the table and excused herself. As she headed for the Ladies' Room, Danny's perpetual grin faded. He gulped some beer and shook his head. "She's kinda uptight, huh?"

I grinned. So he had noticed. "She's different, believe me."

"She really work with you?"

"Yeah."

"How long?"

I started to say a month. That's how long the day had seemed. "Just this morning."

He grinned knowingly at me. "Bet it seems like a month, huh?"

I grinned back. "You're in the wrong business, Danny. You should have been a mind reader."

When I dropped Doreen off at her Jaguar that evening, I asked if she would be all right getting home.

She grinned crookedly. "Not worried about me, are you?"

"Hey, you're my partner. I always worry about my partner."

She looked at me curiously, then nodded. "I'll be just fine."

Back in my apartment, I fed A.B. and booted up my

computer and planned an itinerary for the next day. I
stuck Eisen and Fusco at the end of the list. I needed to
see the fire marshal's report on the fire, to see what incendiary agents the arsonist utilized. Then I wanted to
run down Abe Romero. See where he was on Tuesday
the nineteenth, the night the Hip-Hop burned. I also
wanted to make another run through the storeroom.
Though I had no reason, the more I considered the matter, the more I figured the ticket had to be hidden somewhere in that building.

If we couldn't find the ticket, then the next step was
to hit the pawnshops within walking distance of Sixth
Street and see if anyone remembered Rosey.

I paused, staring at the monitor, disappointed that I
had accomplished so little that day. But then I reminded
myself that maybe I had accomplished more than I
knew for not only had someone tried to slam my head
through a brick wall, someone, maybe that same someone, had tried to leave tire marks on my brand-new
sports coat.

Finally I booted off and plopped down on the couch,
propped my feet on the coffee table and watched a John
Wayne Western on TV.

The jangling of my telephone jerked me from the
exhausted slumber into which I had fallen. It was Janice Coffman-Morrison, my on-again, off-again Significant Other reminding me of our dinner date the next
night.

Next morning, Doreen was waiting for me at my desk when I arrived. She was wearing a dark brown suit. While I'm no expert, it appeared she had applied some makeup.

I uttered a soft curse when I saw her. I was hoping to arrive before her so I could talk to Marty. Jerry Blue's remark about her not liking men still bothered me. I'd just have to catch him another time. I grinned at her. "Ready for another day?"

She pushed to her feet. "I'm ready."

"In just a minute." I reached for the phone and dialed the Austin Police Department. Chief Pachuca was out, so I left my cell number. Doreen looked on curiously, so I explained, "We need to see the fire marshal's report on the fire at the Hip-Hop. See what kind of agent was used to start the fire. It was probably kerosene or gasoline."

Marty stuck his head out of his office. "Tony, before you leave, I need to see you about the International Insurance lawsuit. Bring the file on them."

"Okay." I glanced at Doreen who started to rise and follow me. "Do me a favor. Look up the address of the Texas Star Bar and Grill out in Elgin while I talk to Marty."

She nodded. "Abe Romero?"

"You got it."

After laying out the file on International Insurance and answering Marty's questions, I asked him one of my own. "Yesterday, I talked to Jerry Blue over at Texas Investigations. He told me why they fired your sister-in-law. Said she was hard to work with. She was hostile. But he also made the remark that she didn't like men."

He laughed. "Yeah. He's right. She hates men. Her husband slapped her around. After they divorced, she had a few bad experiences, and now she thinks men should suffer the same fate as a cockroach, to be stomped under the heel of her shoe."

Now her behavior, her demeanor made sense. I didn't agree with it, but at least I knew where she was coming from. I could understand the defensive posture she adopted.

He stopped me when I turned to leave. "How'd she do last night?"

I thought about the previous evening. "All right. She did okay." And the truth was, she had.

To my surprise, Doreen climbed into the pickup without arguing. "Where to first?" she asked.

I glanced at her Jag, then grinned to myself. "You get the address of the bar over in Elgin?"

"Yes." She patted the pocket of her jacket.

"Those dives don't open until around ten or so. I want to go back to Sixth Street first and run down the rest of Rosey's buddies and check the storeroom again. I can't shake the feeling the pawn ticket is hidden in there somewhere."

I've heard about poor old boys so unlucky that they run into accidents intended for someone else. The other edge of that sword is that some people are lucky enough to reap the benefits of an unexpected windfall.

Believe it or not, we got the benefit of a surprise windfall although I didn't really know what to make of it.

Chapter Ten

During the drive down to Sixth Street, Doreen asked, "What happens if we don't find the pawn ticket?"

With a shrug, I replied, "Then we'll just have to rely on legwork."

She paused a moment, then with a hint of satisfaction in her tone, said, "That's what I figured, so last night after I got back to my apartment, I made a list of all of the pawn shops within a dozen blocks of Sixth Street. I figured that was about as far as one of those street bu—I mean, street people would want to walk."

I looked around in surprise. She wore a smug little smile. "Good idea," I replied. "Good idea." Her smile grew wider.

The sidewalks were deserted except for one or two merchants sweeping the walk in front of their places of business. We pulled around the corner of Sixth and San Jacinto into a parking space next to the alley.

Before we climbed from the pickup, I spotted Goofy-foot and Pookie coming out of the alley across the street. They ignored the pickup until I called to them. For a moment, they hesitated, but then recognizing me, angled across the street.

I climbed out to meet them while Doreen remained in the pickup. "Hi, boys." I nodded. "Heading any-where in particular?"

Three or four layers of clothes gave Pookie a robust look, one that his emaciated face instantly disputed. He pointed to the Dumpsters lining the alley. "See what was tossed out last night." He patted his belly.

"Just get up?"

Goofyfoot nodded. "Yep. Slept down at the convention center last night. Good and warm."

I hooked my thumb over my shoulder. "I thought you bunked in the storehouse over there."

Pookie arched a bushy eyebrow. "I ain't staying there no more, not after yesterday."

Goofyfoot grunted. "Reckon he's right. It ain't a good place no more. Getting the wrong crowd of peo-ple hanging in there."

"What do you mean by that?"

Pointing a bony finger at the storehouse, Pookie added,

"Someone done tore the innards out of the place. They musta been looking for something."

"Probably the same one I saw running from it yesterday," Goofyfoot added.

My ears perked up. "Yesterday? What time yesterday?" Absently, I touched my fingers to the Band-Aid on my forehead, hoping we were talking about the same time frame.

He frowned at the urgency in my voice. "I—I don't rightly know," he stammered.

"Think hard, Goofyfoot. Before or after lunch. It's important."

He pondered the question a few moments. I resisted the urge to hurry him. "Let's see. It was before—no, it was after lunch. I'd found me some almost whole Subways down behind Fat Sal's Deli and I was coming back to the storehouse to eat them when some dude in a fancy suit busted out of the door and run across the alley right into the back door of the Red Rabbit."

I stared at him in disbelief. Talk about luck. When I regained my wits, I waved Doreen over.

The two old men watched curiously as she came around the front of the pickup.

"Listen to this," I said to her. "Okay, Goofyfoot. Tell us again what you saw."

He repeated his story. Doreen looked at me in surprise.

I grinned at the old man. "Do you remember what he looked like?"

He scratched at his temple, and I saw flakes of thick dandruff fall to the worn shoulders of the grimy topcoat drooping from his thin frame. "Didn't get that good a look at him except he was a big dude."

"What was he wearing? You remember?" In the back of my mind, I remembered Getdown's remark about the "fancy set of drapes" the dude was wearing.

"Yeah. Like I said, a fancy suit."

"What do you mean, fancy?"

He shrugged. "I don't know. It was blue. That's about all I know. Oh, yeah, he had long hair hanging down his back."

I cut my eyes to Doreen. She nodded.

In my mind, I felt he was telling the truth, but at the same time, when I managed to stumble out into the alley yesterday, no one was around, not the goon who had hit me nor Goofyfoot. "Sounds like the same one we ran into inside the storeroom, but where'd you go? I didn't see you in the alley."

He looked at me as if I'd lost my senses. "Not me. Whatever was happening wasn't none of my business. I got out of there fast."

"But, you're certain it was the Red Rabbit the guy ran into?"

"I should be. We find good stuff out in Buck's Dumpster."

I chuckled and fished a sawbuck from my pocket and offered it to Goofyfoot. "Here. You boys go buy yourself a hot breakfast."

Pookie snatched it from my fingers. "Thanks, Boudreaux. Me and Goofyfoot will sure do that."

As they disappeared around the corner on Sixth Street, with a wry edge in her voice, Doreen remarked, "You know what they'll do with that ten, don't you?"

I laughed. "Buy as much cheap wine as they can and sleep the day away."

Pookie hadn't lied. The storehouse had been ripped apart. Shelves had been torn from the walls and dismantled piece by piece, the contents of the boxes on the shelves were strewn about, and the mattresses were shredded.

Her fists jabbed into her hips, Doreen studied the chaos. "Looks like somebody came back after we left. Do you think they found it?"

"Beats me. If it had been here, I think we would have found it yesterday. I'm guessing they didn't find it either."

"But we can't be sure."

I arched an eyebrow. "You're right. As far as I know, they might be redeeming whatever it was right now. All we can do is keep looking."

A frown wrinkled her forehead. "You mean here?" She gestured to the storeroom.

"No. We might have overlooked it yesterday, but whoever did this—well, I figure this place is clean. You still have that list of pawn shops?"

She patted her pocket. "Right here."

"All right. Let's see Buck first, then we'll start hitting the pawn shops."

Wearing a sparkling new serving jacket, Buck looked up from behind the bar where he was packing beer in the coolers. A single customer sat hunched over the bar, both hands wrapped around a mug of draft beer. Buck grinned. "Hey, Tony, Doreen. How about some coffee?"

"Why not?" I slipped up on a stool and Doreen took the one beside me. I nodded to the jacket. "What's the occasion?"

He tugged on the lapels and grinned. "I decided to give this place some class. Not bad, huh?"

I shrugged. "Not bad."

At that moment, a slight man wearing a black T-shirt and worn jeans held together by holes and slashes, entered and headed for the hallway. Tattoos covered every inch of bare skin. "Hey, Buck."

Buck nodded. "You're late, Clay."

With a shrug, Clay rang his hand over his short-cut hair. "My old lady. I'll get things cleaned up out here." He gestured to the empty beer containers on the tables and floor.

"Make sure you dump the ashtrays too."

Clay grunted.

Grinning broadly despite his missing teeth, Buck poured two cups of coffee and slid them across the bar to us. His eyes lingered on Doreen a few extra seconds.

At that moment, S. S. Thibeaux, whom we'd spotted when we first came down to investigate the torching, pushed through the front door. When he saw us, he jerked to a halt. For a fleeting second, his eyes met Buck's then shifted to me. "Hey, Tony. Saw you come in. How's it going?"

"Can't complain."

Deliberately ignoring Buck, he added, "Stop in and visit when you get a chance."

Although I was well aware of S.S.'s dislike for Buck, I thought nothing of his sudden appearance. As he said, he saw us enter and just stopped in to say hi.

Buck cleared his throat. "What's up? Any progress on Getdown's place?"

I shook my head. "Just getting started." I sipped the coffee. "By the way, you know that storeroom of Getdown's?"

Buck wiped at the bar. "Where all the bums hang out? What about it?"

"Doreen and I were out there yesterday when some guy in a blue business suit jumped us. By the time we got outside, he had disappeared. One of the winos said he saw the guy run in your back door. Just after lunch. You happen to see anyone like that?"

Buck paused, considering the question, at the same time running the tip of his tongue back and forth in the gap between his upper teeth. His eyes darted at Doreen, then back to me. Slowly, he shook his head. "Impossible."

Beside me, I saw Doreen stiffen. "Why impossible?" I asked.

He glanced at the open cooler behind the bar. "I keep the back door locked. Just to keep those bums from stealing me blind," he explained while slamming the cooler door. "And I got me an expensive generator in the back. I sure don't want it hauled away."

I frowned. "Generator?"

"Yeah." He tapped a finger to his temple. "I ain't all that dumb. "Whenever power goes off, I kick that sucker in. I'm the only establishment on the street with lights."

Laughing softly, I replied, "And I bet prices go up, huh?"

His grin split his angular face. "And how. The only ball game in town, so to speak."

Doreen spoke up, her words soft and honeyed. "Could someone have taken a key without you knowing, Buck?"

He leered at her and shook his head. "No way." He patted the key ring on his belt like it was a six-shooter. "This set and one just like it in my vault are the only ones." He leaned toward her, resting his elbows on the bar. "Like I said, ain't no way those bums saw anyone come into my place like that." His brow knit angrily. "Who was it that told you that anyway?"

I shrugged and deliberately lied. "You know how it is, Buck. They all look the same. I don't know."

Doreen persisted. "Maybe one of your employees left it unlocked."

He studied her a moment, then turned on his heel and

headed down a hall toward the rear of the building. He waved for us to follow. I fell in behind Doreen. There were three doors opening off the hall, and just as Doreen passed one, she glanced around at me and nodded to the open door. I glanced in and spotted a small one-gallon fuel container beside a portable generator.

For a moment, I hesitated, but Buck's declaration kept me going. "See." He gestured to the door. "Here's why they couldn't accidentally forget. Two locks. A Master lock on a hasp, and a Sergeant lock in the door. They might forget one, but not two. Any of my employees who leave either one unlocked gets fired." He gave us a satisfied look, but my mind was on the fuel can.

Doreen glanced at me, then smiled at Buck. "I see what you mean."

Buck led the way back to the bar. I stared at his back, unable to shake an overpowering feeling that he was lying through his teeth.

A half-a-dozen garbage bags bulging with trash were piled on the floor in front of the bar. Clay held up his hand. "Need the keys, Buck."

Buck unsnapped the key ring from his belt and tossed it to the slightly built man.

At that moment, my cell phone rang. It was Chief Pachuca. I asked if I could get a copy of the fire marshal's report on the Hip-Hop or if not, just a short interview with the fire marshal.

"Why the fire marshal?"

I watched Buck's eyes when I replied. "I'm curious as to what incendiary agent was used to start the fire."

To my disappointment, Buck didn't react one way or another.

Pachuca promised to get back to me. I punched off and nodded to Buck. "Thanks for the coffee, Buck."

"Anytime. Anytime. Hey, Tony, what's that in—incendiary thing you was talking about? Something to do with the Hip-Hop?"

Then I realized why there was no reaction from Buck. He had no idea what I was talking about. "Yeah. I want to find out what kind of fuel the torch man used to start the fire. You know, gasoline, kerosene—"

Doreen glanced at me, but I kept my eyes on Buck.

His face remained impassive. He shrugged. "Oh."

Clearing her throat, Doreen gestured down the hall. "Before we leave, I need to visit the little girl's room."

"Second door on left," Buck said.

She disappeared down the hall.

Buck leaned across the war. "Nice looking woman. She your squeeze? You two got something going?"

Something going? I shook my head, remembering the stress and aggravation of the previous day. With a straight face, I replied, "Nope, just working together on this case. That's all."

He arched his eyebrows and ran his fingers through

his greasy black hair. "What do you know," he muttered, glancing at the entrance to the hall. "What do you know." He thought for a moment, then said, "I don't suppose you have her phone number, huh?"

Chapter Eleven

Doreen paused with her hand on the door handle of my Silverado and looked across the bed of the pickup at me. "I think he was lying about the back door."

"Oh? What makes you think so?" I climbed behind the wheel.

She opened the door and slid in. "He's a man. Men lie."

I lifted an eyebrow.

Suddenly aware of what she had blurted out, she hastily added. "Present company excepted." With a hint of blush, she continued. "Nothing definite. Body language, I guess. Did you notice he wouldn't look us in the eyes."

I chuckled. "Buck's always been like that. Shifty eyes." With a wry grin, I added, "You must not have noticed, but there were a couple times he was looking you straight in the eye."

She stiffened, then seeing the amusement in my eyes, smiled grimly. "He looks the kind to hit on every woman he sees."

"He is," I replied. "By the way, he wanted your phone number."

Doreen rolled her eyes. "Oh, no."

I chuckled.

She glared at me, but there was a tiny glitter of laughter in her dark eyes. "It isn't funny."

"I know," I replied in mock seriousness. "If you think that wasn't funny, wait until he calls you."

Doreen stared at me in disbelief. "You didn't?"

I laughed. "No. I couldn't do that to anyone. Now, where's that list of pawn shops?"

In the PI business, sometimes you tell the truth, sometimes you lie (although we call it pretext, which obviously sounds much better than lying). The successful PIs have an uncanny knack for knowing when to do which. My knack borders more on the unremarkable than the uncanny, but I figured we'd make more headway at the pawnshops with the truth.

Before we started hitting the shops, I parked in front of Neon Larry's. Leaving the motor running, I hurried inside, looking for S.S.

I'd met S.S. a few years earlier when I stumbled onto

a Chinese Triad smuggling military weapons out of the country. While he was tied to the operation through the tenuous connection of a cousin neck-deep in the operation, S.S. was innocent. But given the mood of the law community and an over-zealous District Attorney, he would have been sent away for years. With a couple judicious omissions in my statement to the police, he dodged indictment.

And he never forgot it.

And I didn't lose any sleep over it.

And given the same circumstances, I'd do it again.

He was a warehouse of street information. From time to time, he had supplied me with snippets of gossip that were of great benefit in regard to various cases.

"He just left. Be in tonight at eight," said Larry, a hollow-eyed carryover from the decade of Flower Children. His gray ponytail hung down to his waist.

By noon, we had canvassed seven pawnshops throughout downtown Austin. Street denizens hocking whatever they could find, hustle, or steal, frequented all of them. Unfortunately, none had paid out the princely sum of $50.00 to any street bum. "Yeah," one owner drawled. "It's usually five, sometimes ten bucks for a watch or whatever. But believe me, if I forked out fifty bucks to a wino, I'd remember. I'd probably call the cops right off."

We grabbed a fast lunch at La Casa on Congress Avenue overlooking the Colorado River. The broad, green river, some hundred feet below, is a spectacular sight, steeped in history. Patches of live oaks dot the rugged white limestone banks sloping down the water's edge. As I downed the last bite of chicken fajitas, my cell rang. It was Chief Pachuca. "I'll save you a trip to the fire marshal, Boudreaux," he said. "They found traces of gasoline."

"Does that help us?" Doreen asked after I told her of the conversation. "Buck had a container of gas in his backroom. I checked."

I grinned. "I figured you would. But don't forget, he also has a generator, which is probably powered by gas." I pushed back from the table. "For all we know, Getdown might have stored gasoline in his backroom."

By 2:00, we had four pawnshops left, all on Congress Avenue south of the river. The first one at which we stopped was Bernie's Pawn, the corner business of a strip mall perched on a bluff overlooking the Colorado River. Bars covered the exterior windows. Inside, the office window, also protected by iron bars, opened into the room.

From behind the window, an overweight woman with sagging jowls, graying hair, and a cigarette dangling from her lips eyed us suspiciously when we entered. I led the way to the window. "Morning. Bernie around?"

Her lips curled. A couple expletives rolled off her lips, and then she added, "Bernie's dead. Six years now."

I shrugged. "You the owner?"

"You a cop?"

"No, ma'am."

"Then I'm the owner, Mrs. Bernie. Bernie was my husband." She squinted through the cigarette smoke at us, probably trying to guess what we were going to pawn. "What in the h—" She hesitated, glanced at Doreen, then apologized. "Sorry. Profanity is a bad habit, but it comes in handy. Kinda like a universal language for some of them I get in here. Now, what can I do for you?"

I showed her my identification and explained, "We're working on a case up on Sixth Street. We were told that a couple weeks back, a wino pawned some object for fifty dollars."

Her eyes narrowed suspiciously. "What was it?"

My hopes soared. At each previous pawnshop, the response to that remark had been a resounding "no," not "what was it?"

I gave her my little-boy-lost smile. "That's what we're trying to find out."

She arched an eyebrow, uttered a couple obscenities and said, "He might have, but he's got a month to redeem it."

Doreen glanced at me, an eyebrow raised at Mrs. Bernie's rough language.

My pulse speeded up, but I tried to keep the excitement from my voice. "Can you tell me what it was?"

Eyeing me narrowly, she replied. "I don't see what harm it can do. It was a glass skull."

Doreen and I exchanged puzzled looks. "A glass skull?"

Mrs. Bernie tapped her forehead. "Yeah. A skull. A glass skull."

Doreen spoke up. "Do you think it would be possible to see it? I've never seen a glass skull."

Mrs. Bernie paused and cocked her head to the side. She spoke with her cigarette between her lips. "What is it about that skull? It something special?"

Doreen and I exchanged puzzled looks once again. "What do you mean?"

She eyed me shrewdly. "You're the second guy today who's come in and asked it about it. I'd figured on doubling my money on it if the old wino don't come back, but maybe I'll be cheating myself at that price seeing there's so much interest in it."

I thought fast, which along with a knack for lying, is essential for a PI, but Doreen beat me to it. "I wonder if it was Edgar who came in, Tony." She turned to Mrs. Bernie. "Edgar works with our company." She held her hand a few inches over her head. "He's about six-two, slender, bald head."

"No." She pointed her cigarette at me. "This one was about same height as your man here, maybe a little taller. Dressed nice. He had black hair in a ponytail and a broken nose."

A broken nose! I suppressed my excitement. With a

shrug, I replied, "That wasn't Edgar. But, can we see the skull?"

She studied us suspiciously, then shrugged. "I don't know what it would hurt. Just a minute."

When she disappeared back into the shelves behind her, Doreen shook her head. "She's a rough one."

I grunted. "On a scale of one to ten, I'd have to say she's at least an eleven."

Doreen smiled. "The guy she mentioned. Do you think he's the same guy who ran out of the storeroom?"

"Ponytail, broken nose. Has to be, which means that—"

At that moment, Mrs. Bernie reappeared with a glass skull in her hands.

"Later," I muttered to Doreen under my breath.

She set the skull on the counter, but kept her hand on it while she hefted her bulk up on the stool. With a suspicious frown on her sagging face, she paused and squinted at me through the cigarette smoke in her eyes. Reaching under the counter, she retrieved a .357 magnum and laid it beside the skull, which she then slid out to me with one hand while the fingers on the other wrapped around the .357.

The skull looked about eight inches from jaw to the crown of the head. Gingerly, I picked it up, immediately surprised not only by its weight, but also the craftsmanship of the skull.

Doreen whistled softly. "It's beautiful."

I wouldn't have called it beautiful, but then I could

see how it could be called that. While I'm no whiz on human anatomy, the skull looked anatomically correct from the forehead down to the lower jaw, which was hinged and functioned just like a human jaw.

The glass was smoky and heavy, heavier than I would have guessed.

Doreen ran a slender finger over the crown of the skull. "I've never seen anything like this," she whispered. Then she looked up at Mrs. Bernie. "Do you know anything about the skull?"

She shook her head. "Naw. I gave the old bum fifty bucks for it 'cause I had never seen nothing like it. You stay in this business long enough, you get to know when something comes along that'll bring in a nice piece of change. I figured on doubling my money, but now I might ask a little more."

I read the tag tied around the lower jaw. "October fifteenth. That's when his time's up?"

"Yeah." She nodded and lit another cigarette.

As I studied the skull, somewhere in the back of my head, I remembered reading about skulls, but crystal skulls not glass skulls. Crystal. I hefted the skull in my hand two or three times, trying to guess how much it weighed. Fifteen to twenty pounds, I figured. Was that why this skull was so heavy? It was made of crystal.

I handed it to Doreen. "Feel how heavy it is. Both hands."

Her eyes grew wide as the weight of the skull caught her by surprise. "It is heavy."

"Well," Mrs. Bernie's cackle broke into my thoughts. "What do you think of it?" She held out her hand for it.

"It's unusual," I replied, sliding the skull back to her. "Really unusual."

By the time we left, I had grown used to Mrs. Bernie's colorful language, at least to the extent that my cheeks didn't blush at every expletive.

We sat in the pickup for several moments studying the pawnshop. "Have you ever heard of crystal skulls?"

Doreen thought a moment. "No. Was that one? It looked like glass to me."

"But you felt how heavy it was."

"Yes, but couldn't it have just been glass. Glass is heavy."

She was right. "Could be." I racked my brain trying to figure out whom we could contact for more information about a crystal skull. Then I thought about Janice Coffman-Morrison and her Aunt Beatrice. Beatrice owned the largest distillery in the state, Chalk Hills, west of Austin. She was richer than the Queen of England, and I had no doubt that every piece of stemware and glassware in her home was leaded crystal. Heaven forbid her fingers touch something as common as glass. I wondered where she purchased her crystal.

I continued staring at the pawnshop. The left side of my brain shifted to the right as I thought about the black-haired goon with the broken nose.

"Is something wrong?"

"Huh?" I looked around at her. "Oh. I was thinking about the guy who paid Mrs. Bernie a visit earlier today."

She frowned. "What about him?"

I pointed to the pawnshop. "I got a feeling he's coming back."

A flicker of alarm raced across her face. "Back? When?"

"Tonight."

"Are you sure?"

"Nope." I shook my head. "But I'd give odds on it." I paused, then added. "Stop and think about it. Chances are this is the guy in the storeroom, and maybe he finally located the skull today. For some reason he wants it. Obviously, he hasn't had any more luck that we have in finding the pawn ticket. That means, if he wants the skull, then he's got to get it by some other means."

"You think he's going to try to steal it?"

"Yeah." I nodded. "Tonight."

Her eyes grew wide momentarily. "So what are we going to do?"

After pondering her question several moments, I replied, "First, I'll inform Mrs. Bernie of our suspicions and have her make sure her alarm system is on. Then I'll tell Chief Pachuca about it. He can have the shift officers keep an eye on her place tonight, and last, I'll be where I can watch. Maybe find out where this scumbag holes up." I opened the door. "Be right back."

I paused at the entrance to the pawnshop, dismayed when I failed to spot an alarm system.

Mrs. Bernie frowned when she saw me. "Forget something?"

Quickly, I explained that someone had murdered the wino who had pawned the skull, and that there were others who wanted it. "I might be wrong, but I think he'll try to break in tonight. I'll inform the police. I was going to remind you to set your alarm system, but I don't see one." I glanced around the shop.

She studied me with amusement. "Oh, my alarm system will be on. It's always on." She glanced at the floor at her feet. "Ain't that right, Max?"

Through the barred window, I could see no lower that her chest, but the raw growl that came from below the window was unmistakable. After colorfully describing any would-be thief's ancestry, she added. "Any idiot what tries to break in to my shop will be sorry."

When I climbed in the pickup, I glanced at Doreen. "We'll head back to the office, and I'll contact Pachuca."

Doreen studied me a moment. "Can I come tonight?"

I looked around in surprise. For a second or so, I just stared at her. "Well, sure. I just didn't figure that— well—that you wanted to."

"When I told you I wanted to learn this business, Tony, I was serious. I'm not some flighty bimbo." She started to say more, then decided against it.

Maybe I had been mistaken about her. "Fine with me."

I started up the Silverado and headed north on Congress. We caught a red light at Second Street. When it changed, we met a blue Miata heading south. I spotted it just in time to recognize my on-again, off-again Significant Other, Janice Coffman-Morrison, one of Austin's poor little rich girls.

She honked and waved. I returned the salutation, glancing in the side mirror in time to see her almost break her neck looking around when she realized that I had a woman in the pickup with me. I rolled my eyes. I would be getting a phone call later today. Then I muttered a curse, suddenly remembering that Janice and I had a previous date for tonight. Now I was going to have to break it.

"Someone you know?"

With a rueful grin, I nodded. "A friend. We go out together from time to time."

When it comes to understanding women, I'm the best checker player in the world. And once again, I was mistaken. I didn't have to wait until later for Janice's call. My cell rang immediately.

Janice's voice was sweet, but I detected a massive dose of poison in it. "Hello, Tony."

"Hey, Janice. What's up?" Remembering the crystal skull, I added. "I was about to give you a call."

"Well, here I am," she replied. "What was so important?"

"About tonight, I—"

She interrupted. "Why don't you come over early for cocktails before we go to dinner?"

I grinned at the tactful way she was beating around the bush, then drew a deep breath. "I have to beg off tonight, Janice. I've got to work."

"What? But, we have a date."

Hastily I tried to explain. "I know, but I just found out. I've got to run a surveillance tonight."

Acidly, she replied, "Who are you going to run a surveillance on, that—that—that woman in the pickup with you?"

I rolled my eyes, wondering how I had managed to get myself in such a predicament. "No. She's a new PI Marty hired. We're working on an arson case on Sixth Street."

Doreen arched an eyebrow at me.

"I bet you are."

"It's the truth, Janice. I promise it is."

"I can't believe you would do this to me, Tony."

Frustrated, I struggled to explain. "Janice, I'm not doing anything to you. Believe me."

She sniffed. "Well, I don't believe you. I don't care if I ever see you again."

"But Janice—"

She didn't even say good-bye. She slammed her cell phone shut.

After I punched off, Doreen's eyes glittered with amusement. "Your girlfriend?"

I nodded. "Was."

"Problems?"

"What do you think?"

She laughed. "I think she's jealous."

"You're crazy."

Chapter Twelve

Doreen remained silent. On impulse I turned down Sixth Street.

"I thought we were going back to the office."

Slowing the pickup, I scanned the sidewalks and alleys. "Watch that side."

"For what?"

"Goofyfoot, Pookie, any of the old winos." When we stopped at the first signal light, I quickly hit the automatic dial on my cell phone for Beatrice Morrison, figuring if I waited until Janice vented her spleen to her aunt, I might never learn the Morrison source of lead crystal.

Beatrice's male secretary answered. Normally, rustic yokels like me can never speak to the grand dame of Texas Distilleries, but since I dated her niece, the secretary recognized my name and put me through.

Beatrice didn't particularly care for the idea of her only relative dating a bourgeois and ignorant Cajun, but she tolerated me for Janice's sake. The only time Aunt Beatrice deigned to socialize with me was when she wanted a pot of my gumbo for one of her dinners.

"Hello, Tony," she replied with a big dose of reservation in her tone.

"How are you today, Aunt Beatrice?" Although she had requested me to address her as such, I knew the words coming from my lips rankled her, and each time I went to confession, I had to admit I enjoyed rankling her like that.

"I'm well, thank you."

Behind us a horn honked. The light had changed. I moved across the intersection, and as I pulled into a Loading Zone, I said, "I hate to impose, Aunt Beatrice, but I figured you, of all people in Austin, could give me the name of someone who is an expert on leaded crystal."

My request took her aback momentarily. "Crystal?" I heard a hint of disbelief in her tone. "Are you buying crystal?"

"No, ma'am. I just need to talk to someone who is very knowledgeable in the field." In the rearview mirror, I spotted a police cruiser turning the corner.

Phone at my ear, I hastily climbed out, fumbled for my magnetized sign, slapped it on the door, and leaned casually against the fender of the Silverado as Beatrice replied, "We purchase all of our crystal from Tower

Jewelers. J. C. Towers is the connoisseur of crystal in Texas. All of our crystal comes from him." In the background, I heard a door close. She hesitated. "Oh, hello, Janice."

I heard Janice ask. "Am I interrupting anything, Aunt Beatrice?"

"No, dear. I'm just talking to Tony."

I spoke up. "Thank you for the information, Aunt Beatrice. And if you don't mind, may I speak with Janice?"

She must have offered the receiver to Janice for I heard my poor little rich girl snap, "I don't want to talk to him ever again."

Now, I can't swear for certain, but I thought that I detected a hint of smug satisfaction in Beatrice's voice when she replied, "I'm sorry, Tony. But she never wants to speak to you again."

Shaking my head, I punched off just as the police cruiser stopped beside me. The shotgun window hissed down and the officer leaned over. "What are you doing down here, Boudreaux? Slumming?"

I recognized the grinning face of Frank Watson. "Trying to make a buck, Frank. Hey, you seen any of the street guys around—Pookie, Downtown, any of them?"

"Over in the alley. A couple are sleeping in a box behind a Dumpster." He glanced at the pickup. "That's yours?"

"Yeah?"

With a suspicious grin, he asked, "When did you get in the delivery business?"

"Hey, you know how it is with PIs, Frank. We have to have all kinds of sidelines just to make half of what you rich cops make."

He sneered at me.

"Which Dumpster?" I asked.

"Behind the Red Rooster."

As Doreen and I headed for the alley, I brought her up to date on what I had learned from Beatrice. "When we get back to the office, I'll get in touch with this Towers guy, and we'll get in to see him."

A frown knit her brows. "About the skull?"

"Yeah. I don't know. In the back of my mind, I think I've heard or read something about crystal skulls, but for the life of me, I can't remember what.'

We turned down the alley, and I spotted Clay, Buck's handyman, hauling out garbage from the Red Rooster. He was wearing the same black T-shirt and threadbare jeans he had worn the day before.

I nodded, but he ignored us.

"Friendly sort," Doreen muttered sarcastically.

"Probably spaced out."

After Clay dumped the garbage and locked the door to the Red Rooster behind him, I spotted a pair of worn-out Nike running shoes protruding from a cardboard box behind the Dumpster. I squatted and peered into the box, but the old man was bundled in a GI greatcoat held together by dirt, and his knitted toboggan mask only showed his closed eyes and thin lips from which the drool had soaked into the cardboard in a spreading damp stain.

I tapped the sole of his shoes with my knuckles. After a moment, he stirred and grunted. I rose and stepped back. "Pookie?"

From the box came an almost unintelligible reply. "Not here."

"Who's in there? Goofyfoot? Spryo? Downtown?"

Moments later, the running shoes began moving and the grimy bundle began sliding out. The brown mask finally emerged and two phlegmy eyes squinted up at me. A dirt-stained hand pulled the mask up.

I recognized Spryo.

He grunted when he recognized me. He glanced at Doreen. "You looking for something?"

"Yeah. You."

The emaciated old man managed to stagger to his feet. "Me. What for? I ain't done nothing."

"I'm looking for a man. It's worth twenty bucks. The guy's got a black ponytail, busted nose, wears fancy suits."

He glanced suspiciously at Doreen and then back to me. "Ain't seen him. He a regular from around here?"

I shrugged. "No idea, but he's been around the last few days." I glanced up and down the alley. "If you run across Downtown or the others, pass word on."

Spryo scratched his sunken chest, no doubt rearranging his colonies of lice. "Who is this dude?"

"I'm not sure. Just don't get nosy. If you see him, let me know. Don't get involved with him. He might be dangerous."

Spryo's eyes narrowed. "He the one who kilt Rosey?"

I held my hands out to the side. "No idea. He might have nothing to do with anything. I just want to talk to him."

He nodded and began rubbing his belly slowly. "I'll run down the boys for you." He narrowed his eyes as he rolled his shoulders and dragged the tip of his tongue over his dried and cracked lips with great lassitude.

One thing I had to admit about those tenants of the street, they had perfected the use of body language. At the moment his eyes and face and sagging shoulders reflected intense exhaustion, ravenous hunger, and acute thirst. With a chuckle, I handed him five bucks. "Here. This will help you find them."

Suddenly, the lassitude, the hunger, the thirst vanished as Spryo grabbed the five and scurried down the alley.

Doreen chuckled. "That perked him up."

"The magic healing power of money." I glanced around. "Now, let's get back to the office."

Just before we reached the end of the alley, the squeal of tires and the roar of a powerful engine jerked me around.

Roaring toward us was the snarling grill of the same Lincoln that had taken a swipe at me the day before. I grabbed Doreen's arm. "Run!"

We darted around the corner of the building only seconds before the Lincoln slammed into the corner, shearing off a chunk of brick, bouncing over the curb, ripping up a parking meter, and fishtailing into the alley across the street.

But not before I got his license number.

Chapter Thirteen

My luck was running true to form. When I ran the license number through the DMV, I discovered it belonged to a 2003 Lexus that had reported the plates stolen.

I muttered a curse. "That's twice that joker has tried to get me," I told Marty. "I might not be a Sherlock Holmes, but I'm smart enough to figure there's more involved here than just a case of arson."

Marty pursed his lips and glanced at Doreen briefly. Fat folds of a frown creased his forehead. "Look, Tony. We're not in the business of getting ourselves knocked off. We leave that to the cops. I'll bill Joe Sillery for what we've done and refund the rest of his retainer."

Well aware of Marty's penchant for money, I knew this decision had been a tough one for him. And I'd be lying if I said at first it gave me sort of a warm feeling, which began cooling when I realized his concern was not for me, but his wife's sister. His wife would never let him have a moment's piece if anything happened to her little sister.

"Forget that, Marty. Whoever torched the place killed Rosey. I want to nail that slime."

"Rosey? But he was just a bum."

Whatever warm feeling was left in my chest turned to ice as my boss once again donned his tried-and-true insensitive self. "He might have been a bum, but he never hurt anybody. He didn't deserve what he got. Somebody's going to pay."

At that moment, my cell rang. It was Danny O'Banion. The information he provided eliminated Patsy Fusco and Mossy Eisen.

"Fusco had been interested, but last month, Jack Drapper, who headed up the South Side in San Antonio sort of woke up dead one morning, and Fusco took over his territory. Eisen ain't interested. When Joe Vasco in New Orleans heard Eisen had been asking questions, he suggested Eisen be satisfied with Atlanta." Danny chuckled. "Eisen ain't no genius, but he ain't stupid either."

After hanging up, I shared the information with Doreen who then reminded me we had still not interviewed Abe Romero.

I glanced at my watch. "It's after four. We'll do it tomorrow. Why don't you go home and catch a short nap. Bernie's closes at nine. I'll meet you here about eight."

After Doreen left, I called J. C. Towers, Texas's Connoisseur of Crystal according to Dame Beatrice, and set up a meeting at 10:00 the next morning.

During the drive to my apartment on Payton Gin Road, I tried to sort my thoughts, but the clamor and din of heavy traffic was overpowering.

As usual, before I was halfway home, I swore I was going to find a place closer in; as usual, I knew I wouldn't. Austin is typical of growing cities all over the country. As income grows, people move to newer, more upscale neighborhoods. Lower income citizens move into to their vacated house, just like a chain. Somewhere down the chain comes slums, which are usually concentric rings expanding from the downtown area.

When I finally closed the apartment door behind me, I made for the kitchen and popped the top on an soft drink and downed several gulps.

A.B. rubbed up against my ankles, so I nuked him some milk and filled his other bowl with nuggets. I wandered into the living room where I flipped on the TV and plopped down on the couch.

Staring unseeing at the TV, I tried to put my thoughts into some semblance of order and priority, which wasn't too difficult. Whoever burned the Hip-Hop killed Rosey to cover the murder and was trying to do the same to me. The only explanation, the only motive that made sense was the crystal skull.

At that moment, the phone rang. It was Janice. I rolled my eyes, bracing myself for another fusillade of browbeating, but to my surprise, butter, to paraphrase an old cliché, could have melted in her mouth. "I'm sorry about today, Tony. I just didn't think. I apologize."

I was speechless. Seldom did Janice Coffman-Morrison apologize to anyone. Royalty never stoops to contrition. I stammered. "I understand. Don't worry about it."

"What about tomorrow night? Are you busy then?" I heard a trace of suspicion in her tone.

Right then I made up my mind, I was not going to be busy. "No. How about dinner tomorrow night? Same place, the boardroom at the Ritz-Carlton?"

"Wonderful. Cocktails out here at eight?"

"See you then."

For several moments, I sat slumped on the couch, a sappy grin on my face. Slowly, my thoughts went back to the crystal skull.

On impulse, I slipped behind my computer and went online where I ran a search on crystal skulls. To my surprise, I discovered a plethora of speculation and supposition.

I spent the next few hours reading about the ancient crystal skulls, and as I read, my skepticism grew.

According to the information I pulled up, there were at least six crystal skulls that had been uncovered in the last two hundred years. Their ages theoretically ranged from five thousand to thirty-six thousand years, but what was so perplexing was that the technology used to carve the skulls from crystal has only been available in the last few decades. As I read, I jotted a few questions for Mister Towers.

Most of the stuff was Internet garbage as far as I was concerned, but then I stumbled across a piece of information that arrested my attention faster than an irate cop can slam a perp up against the wall—an article written by a J. Adkins-Manor.

The article focused on one skull, the Nelson-Vines Crystal Skull, which was not only anatomically correct but also had a movable jawbone. That was not as surprising as the next statement, which stated that from a technical standpoint, not even today's most talented sculptors or engineers could duplicate the Nelson-Vines Crystal Skull. And it was thousands of years old!

Suddenly, I sat up, staring at the screen. The skull at Bernie's had a moveable jaw. Could it be the Nelson-Vines Skull?

A sudden barrage of theories bombarded my brain. Had another skull been discovered? Or was this the same skull, stolen to be held for ransom only to be lost? What was the value of an only-one-of-its-kind skull to a serious collector? Enough to kill for? I shook my head. Stupid question.

To my added surprise, I learned that select groups the world over collected, even worshipped crystal skulls, a behavior, if you think about it, no different than worshipping some of the material idols many celebrate today.

The jangling of the telephone cut into my thoughts.

Still reading the screen, I picked up the receiver. "Boudreaux here."

"Tony. It's me, Doreen. Where are you? I've been waiting in the parking lot for thirty minutes."

I glanced at my watch and muttered a curse. "Sorry. Be right there." I turned back to my computer. Hastily I sent an e-mail query to J. Adkins-Manor, questioning the possibility of a second Nelson-Vines Crystal Skull.

I reached the parking lot just before nine. She suggested we take her Jaguar. "After all, we've used your pickup the last couple days. Someone might recognize it."

For a moment, I hesitated. So what? Everyone knew my truck. But then, I shrugged. What could it hurt? Besides, it had been years since I'd ridden in a Jaguar.

While the low-slung Jaguar makes me feel like my rear was dragging the ground, I couldn't argue with the luxury of the sports car with its soft leather seats and burled dash nor the boost to the ego of riding in such a sleek car with the top down despite the nip in the air.

During the drive down Lamar and Guadalupe to Congress Avenue, more than one head turned to look after us. When we stopped at the signal light at Congress and Tenth Street, a car pulled up beside us and one head too many turned to look.

It was Janice in her little Miata, and when she spotted

me, her face turned into a slab of ice. Before I could open my mouth, the light changed, and she shot away.

Doreen frowned and glanced at me. "Hey, wasn't that your little friend we saw today?"

"Yeah," I replied weakly, leaning back and staring into dark night overhead. "And *was* is the definitive verb here."

The strip mall that housed Bernie's Pawnshop was a couple hundred feet long, in front of which grew a neatly trimmed privet hedge. A used car lot was adjacent to the strip, and in the rear of the office were parked a dozen or so automobiles with tarps draped over them against the weather until they could be refurbished and placed in the front lot.

I instructed Doreen to pull into the rear, where we parked beside one of the cars. After Doreen raised the Jag's top, I pulled one end of a tarp over the Jag, leaving the front window and hood uncovered. "You watch from here. I'll go around to the other end of the building and find a place by the bridge."

"What if I see someone?"

"Just honk, three times, but stay in the car and keep the doors locked."

The Congress Avenue Bridge serves as a sleeping spot for transients although most of them find spots in downtown alleys closer to food and drink. Except for one or two, I had the bridge to myself. I found a spot behind some shrubs where I could see the rear of the buildings plus have a good view of the bridge as well as the trail leading down to the river. I settled down to wait, rehashing the events of the last couple days.

The river rolled past a hundred feet below at the base of a steep slope covered with trees and shrubs.

Time dragged. Several times, I heard the sound of feet on rock. Occasional murmurs drifted up the slope, but after a few moments, the sounds ceased as a transient found himself a snug spot for the night. I yawned, beginning to wonder if I had swung at a wild pitch.

Suddenly from below, metal against rock jerked me awake. A skiff had touched the rocky shoreline. I blinked against the darkness, peering into the night.

Then came the scrape of footsteps. I hunched closer to the ground although I knew my outline was lost in the shadows cast by the bridge. Minutes passed, and then I heard labored breathing. Seconds later, a dark shadow appeared on the trail.

From time to time the shadow paused, then continued. As it grew closer to the pawnshop, it dropped into a crouch, trying to blend with the shadows cast by the trees and shrubs lining the trail.

Abruptly, the shadow darted out of my sight to the rear of the building.

I crept closer. Despite the occasional traffic on the bridge, I heard the clink of metal on metal as he jimmied the rear door. I paused behind a live oak, its lowest limbs about five or six feet above the ground.

I moved forward in time to see a figure step through the door and close it after him. That's when I reached for my cell phone. I had arranged with Pachuca to report in if I spotted anything that night. "Don't go overboard, Boudreaux," he had insisted. "You've no jurisdiction. You see something, call in. We'll have a cruiser right there." And I had no argument with that. I was no hero.

Quickly, I punched in the number of the police station.

In the next instant, a terrified scream followed by the enraged snarls of a very angry dog cut through the rumble of traffic on the bridge.

Suddenly the door burst open and a dark figure leaped out, screaming and trying to fight off Max, the monster dog. The flailing shadow scrambled in my direction.

On his heels, snarling and snapping, came the Rottweiler, and I could swear I saw the moonlight glittering off his talonlike teeth.

Grinning, I pressed up against the trunk of the tree. Moments later, the screaming man raced past with the enraged dog growling and snapping at his heels. I tried to get a look at his face, but the limbs of the live oak sagged too low.

Suddenly, the dog slid to a halt and turned back to me.

I froze, and then a voice in my head screamed do something, Boudreaux. Do something.

And I did. Just as the dog leaped at me, I swung up on the live oak limbs. Something caught the tail of my jacket, yanking at me. I clung to the limb for dear life as the snarling dog hung in the air momentarily.

A loud clatter of rocks and a scream of pain sounded from down the slope.

Without warning, the dog released my coat and, barking and yapping, raced down the slope. I skittered several feet higher into the tree, peering into the darkness below.

I heard the poor guy fall once or twice more, the dog snarl and yap, the guy scream, a moment of silence; then he'd scream again and the dog would yap again. Moments later, I heard a splash in the water.

That's when I dropped to the ground. I hesitated, staring at the blood on the white rocks at my feet. Suddenly from below, I heard the frantic yapping of the dog.

I wasted no time sprinting back to the Jaguar.

Just as I jumped in and slammed the door, an infuriated Rottweiler slammed into the window.

"Go, go, go," I shouted.

The Jag leaped forward while Doreen screamed, "He's scratching my car."

"Then get us out of here before that monster bites off a tire."

Chapter Fourteen

As we pulled onto the bridge, I told her to drop me off on Sixth Street. "Why can't I go?" There was a hint of defiance in her tone.

"I don't know how late I'll be."

She grunted. "Hey, I'm a big girl. In case you have noticed, I can stay out after dark."

Suddenly, she hit the brakes and brought the Jag to a screeching halt in the middle of the Congress Street Bridge.

Four vehicles had piled up, spilling gas over the bridge and closing it down. Traffic piled up behind us. We were in the outside lane, but Doreen managed to work to the inside, then made a quick U-turn and headed back in the direction from which we had come.

114

We had wasted thirty minutes in the traffic jam. Fifteen minutes later, we turned down Sixth Street.

Still complaining, she pulled over to the curb. "I still don't see why I can't go with you."

I climbed out and closed the door. "With all these cowboys and zombies on the street, you draw too much attention."

My remarks were punctuated by two leering punks who whistled and shouted for her to "dump the dude and come with us."

"See what I mean?"

She smiled becomingly, and although the flashing neon signs suffused her face with red and orange, I could have sworn I saw a blush creep into her cheeks. "All right. I'll see you tomorrow."

After she drove away, I inspected the back of my coat. I muttered a curse when I saw the eight-inch-long rip. Two days, two coats.

I shook my head and looked up and down the bustling street. I planned to canvas it, searching for three men; S.S., behind the bar at Neon Larry's; another with fresh dog bites; and a third in a pinstripe suit, sporting a ponytail and a nose spread over his face.

S.S. was first.

Neon Larry's was jumping.

Blue smoke filled the dimly lit club. Against a far wall, a mismatched four-piece combo banged out an unrecognizable tune. Two dozen tables, all filled, were spread around the room. I slid onto an empty stool at the bar.

Wearing a Neon Larry's T-shirt over a long sleeve shirt and a do-rag, S.S. gave no sign of recognition when he spotted me. He wiped the bar in front of me. "What'll it be, pal?" He pursed his lips.

"Draft beer."

Moments later, he returned with the beer. "Two bucks."

I handed him a five. After making change, he tossed the $3.00 on the counter. "Anything else?"

"Yeah. Where's the john?"

He pointed down the hall and turned back to another customer. I set the beer on the $3.00 to mark my spot and headed for the men's room, which coincidentally just happened to share a thin wall with the storeroom behind the bar.

Pushing the unpainted door open to the john, I flipped on the light and stood patiently as a dozen resident water roaches scampered across the walls and disappeared into the cracks in the corners. I locked the door behind me and waited.

Moments later, a voice came through a pencil-sized hole in the wall about eye level. "What's up?"

"The Hip-Hop was burned last week. I need a name or two that can point me in the right direction of the torch man."

There was a hesitation, then S.S. replied, "Wanda

Darcy. Thinks she's a hot singer. Hangs out at the Blue Light with all them other weirdos doing that Black Metal stuff."

"What's her connection?"

"I ain't sure. When I heard some talk about the Hip-Hop, her name came up."

"One more question. Buck Topper and Calvin Engels. Their names mentioned with it?"

"Engels ain't got the guts. Besides, he can do his business on the street. He don't need no club."

"What about Topper?"

S.S. sneered. He hated Buck Topper. I never learned exactly why, but rumor had it Buck had cheated S.S. out of over a hundred thousand, the very hundred thousand he used to purchase the Red Rabbit four years earlier.

More than once when S.S. and I were alone, he had regaled me with the exact methods he would gleefully use to carve up the man. "He ain't no good, but there ain't nothing out there about him and the fire. I wish there was. I'd have made sure the cops got hold of it, but there ain't."

"Thanks."

Back at the bar, I finished my beer, slid a ten under the three bucks for a tip, and sauntered out on the sidewalk. I headed for the Blue Light on the next block, considering the information I had garnered from S.S. For the present, I dropped Buck Topper and Calvin Engels down a few notches on my primary list of suspects.

I'm not going to pretend I understand or enjoy the deafening music bouncing off the walls of the Blue Light. You can almost feel the floor vibrate from the incessant pounding of the Black Metal music that is a cacophonous cross between rap, reggae, and ragtime.

Standing on stage in front of the combination of an electric guitar and keyboard following the primitive rhythm pounded out by the drums was a woman wearing her black hair in spikes. Her eyes were closed, and her black-cloaked body swayed back and forth to the unsteady beat of the music, uttering words understood only by those zonked with the current drug of choice. I guessed her to be in her late thirties or early forties, and doing her best to appear twenty.

Wanda Darcy.

My casual dress was out of place in a club filled with black eyes, white makeup, and rainbow-colored mohawks. I slid on a stool at the bar and glanced around self-consciously.

While the group continued to pummel the walls with its jarring chords, Wanda stumbled off the stage and plopped down at a table. She lifted an almost empty mug of beer to her lips and drained it.

Quickly, I bought two mugs of beer and set one on the table in front of her. She looked up through bleary eyes. "Who are you?"

"An admirer. I heard you sing."

She studied me a moment, then nodded and gestured to the chair across the table.

As I sat, I glanced at the musicians. The long-haired guitar strummer eyed me suspiciously. I smiled and nodded.

Wanda sipped the beer, spilling some down her chin and neck. "Admirer, huh?" She grinned smugly, her eyelids fluttering between closed and half-closed.

"Yes, but that isn't why I'm here." I handed her a business card. "I'm looking for someone, and if you can help me, it's worth a hundred bucks."

Her eyes grew wide, then quickly drooped to half-closed. Without looking at the card, she slipped it down the front of her blouse. "Who you looking for?"

The band had stopped playing and put their instruments down. The skeletal guy on the keyboard was eyeing me with the same suspicion as the guitar strummer. The third one, the drummer, just sat staring over our heads with a dreamy smile on his face.

"Someone who can give me information on the fire down at the Hip-Hop last week."

She gulped another swallow of beer and laughed drunkenly. "Is that all? Hey, everybody knows about that."

The two musicians started toward me. They were both about my size, probably not in as good condition as I, but they were fifteen years younger and that made a difference.

Keeping one eye on the approaching musicians and the other on Wanda, I quickly replied, "Do you know someone who can tell me about it? Like I said, it's worth a hundred bucks."

She was beginning to slur her words. "Sure I can. Where's the money?"

By now, the two cold-eyed bozos were three tables away. "What's the name?"

She leaned forward, but before she could give me a name, one of the men grabbed her shoulder and glared at me. "What's going on here?"

With the mug in hand, I rose and amiably explained. "Nothing to get upset about, friend. I'm looking into the fire down at the Hip-Hop last week so I've been talking to people up and down the street. It's worth a hundred dollars for information."

Wanda jumped to her feet and knocked the keyboard player's hand away. "You get out of here, Jojo. That's my money. He asked me first." She slapped at him and missed.

And I knew I was in trouble when Jojo slapped her back. He didn't miss. She spun around and fell across a table, overturning it.

"Hey, what's going on over there?" the bartender yelled, slurring his words.

His eyes fixed on mine, Guitar Strummer shouted back, "We got a nosy cop over here trying to cause trouble."

"Ain't nobody, not even a cop coming in my place and causing no trouble," the bartender exclaimed, staggering around the end of the bar and attempting to block my exit through the front door.

I muttered a soft curse to myself. This was one situation I was not going to be able to talk my way out of. Off to my right, a few tables away, I spotted a hall leading to the restrooms and the alley. Two of the tables by the hall entrance were occupied.

I just hoped there were not two locks on this door like Buck Topper had on his.

"Look boys, I'm not a cop. I'm a private investigator hired to look into the fire by the insurance company."

The bartender snorted. "That's even worse. You insurance companies are getting rich off us little guys." He reached into his hip pocket and pulled out a slapjack.

I didn't hesitate.

I kicked the table into the knees of the musicians, threw the beer in the bartender's eyes, and darted for the hallway, deliberately grabbing one of the customers at each of the two occupied tables and yanking them to the floor as I shot past.

Behind me exploded an uproar of curses, running feet, shrill screams, and chilling threats. Just as I reached the restroom door, it opened. I didn't slow down. I hit the door and whoever was standing behind it.

Someone yelped in surprise, and then a woman's scream cut through the clamor and clangor with a stream of profanities that my *Grandpere* Moise would have knocked me to the floor if I had spewed them.

The rear door was closed, but fortunately unlocked.

Unfortunately, however, the screen door was locked; having no choice, I simply ran through it.

I burst into the alley and turned east.

Behind me, the screen door slammed open and voices pursued me. When I hit the sidewalk, I headed for Sixth Street. It was after 2:00 and the bars were closing down. Only a few partygoers remained on the street. I turned the corner and immediately ran into half-a-dozen bald-headed men wearing red robes. I don't know if they Muslims, Buddhists, Hindus, Wiccans, or Hare Krishnas. All I know is that we went down in a tangle of arms, legs, and robes.

I managed to extricate myself from the web of limbs and clothing and dashed across the street just as Guitar Strummer and the bartender skidded around the corner and stumbled over the sprawled figures on the sidewalk.

As soon as I turned the corner on Trinity Street, I pressed up against the building and, gasping for breath, peered around the corner. The robed men were shouting and waving their arms at Guitar Strummer and the bartender.

I grinned to myself. It couldn't have happened to more deserving men.

Suddenly, Guitar Strummer shouted and pointed at me.

Cursing to myself, I raced up the hill. On impulse, I turned down another alley and hid behind a Dumpster. Moments later, the two men sprinted past, and I quickly scurried down the alley to Neches Street.

Pausing in the alley at Neches, I looked up and

down the street. Suddenly shouts from behind jerked me around.

Those two bozos were like bloodhounds.

Just as I turned to run, a car honked. Half-a-block away, a cherry-red Jaguar pulled away from the curb and raced toward me.

Chapter Fifteen

As we cut over to Guadalupe, Doreen explained, "I parked up the street and watched from inside The Lighthouse. I spotted you come out of Neon Larry's and go into the Blue Light. When you ran into all those monks or whatever they were, I figured it was time to give you a hand."

I laughed. "I'm glad you did. Those bozos had some bad hurt on their minds."

"Learn anything?"

"No. Another name, but those guys interrupted before we could talk."

The headlights from oncoming vehicles lit her face like a strobe. I saw a smug grin on her lips. Keeping her eyes fixed forward, she said, "Well, I had some luck."

I frowned at her.

She continued. "While I was waiting in The Lighthouse next to Fat Sal's, a guy hurried in holding his hand to his chest. He disappeared into the rear of the bar."

My frowned deepened.

And then she added. "He was Asian, and he was dripping wet. Could have come out of the river."

I could have kissed her, but I resisted. "The Lighthouse, huh?"

"Yeah. Know it?"

"Jimmy Wong owns it, and the Devil's Den on the other side of Fat Sal's. Rumor is you can buy anything you want in The Lighthouse. If it isn't there, then it's two doors down."

"You think he has any connection to the fire?"

I leaned back in the seat and stared at what few stars managed to glitter their way through the hazy glow of city lights. "He could. Any of the bar owners could be involved."

We pulled into the parking lot outside the office and parked beside my Silverado. "How do you mean?"

"They're all hustlers. That's their business down there. There isn't one who wouldn't jump at the chance to pick up another bar."

"Do they really make that much from those bars?"

"It isn't just the booze and entertainment. Most of those characters have several businesses going: prostitution, drugs, hot items. You name it, they've got it.

They pull in a hundred thousand a year easy. Cash for the most part. That's why the clubs change hands every few years. The smart ones get in, make their bundle, and then bail out. But, I can't believe any of them would deliberately torch the place. Why destroy something you would have to rebuild?" I shook my head. "I still think it was done to cover up Rosey's murder.

"So now what?"

"Now, we get a few hours sleep. We've an appointment with J.C. Towers at ten in the morning. I want to stop by The Lighthouse and the pawnshop before we see him."

Before I climbed into bed just after 3:00, I checked my e-mail, hoping for a reply from J. Adkins-Manor.

Nothing.

At 3:15, the phone rang, and a hushed voice whispered, "This the guy down at the Blue Light tonight?"

Groggy from sleep and exhaustion, I mumbled, "Who's this?"

"Wanda Darcy."

Instantly, I was awake. "Yeah, yeah, it's me. Where are you?"

"That don't matter. You still got the hundred bucks?"

"Yeah. It's yours. Just put me in touch with someone who knows about the fire, and I'll get the hundred to you."

"No. We got to meet."

The hackles on the back of my neck bristled. I didn't want any more to do with those bozos in her musical entourage, but I hated to pass up such an opportunity. "Where?"

"The parking lot at Neches and Ninth Street?"

I knew the spot. "When?"

"Thirty minutes?"

"Can't make it. Earliest I can get there is five. It's still dark then. What about your friends?"

"They ain't part of it."

You bet, I told myself. "Five all right?"

"Yeah. I guess it'll have to do."

After hanging up, I dressed quickly. She might be playing me straight, but I wasn't stupid enough to take a chance.

By 4:00 a.m., I was situated on the roof of a warehouse across Ninth Street from the parking lot, on which a dozen or so automobiles were parked.

The streets were deserted except for an occasional partygoer wandering the streets trying to remember where he left his car. Overlooking the parking lot from the south was a sagging flophouse, all windows dark except for two.

I tightened my jacket about me against the nip in the air.

At 4:15, three dark figures crossed Neches Street and entered the flophouse. Moments later, one of the lights flicked off.

I waited, and then four figures emerged and headed for the parking lot. Three of them disappeared among the parked cars while the fourth waited out in the open.

"Good try," I muttered softly. "But no gold ring this time, Wanda."

At 5:30, one of the figures emerged and waved for the others to join him. Though their words were unintelligible, their angry voices carried across the lot. Moments later, the three bozos stormed away, and Wanda headed back to her apartment.

When her light came on, I scrambled down the fire escape and hurried across the parking lot.

The stench of mold and unwashed bodies slapped me in the face when I entered the dilapidated building. The night clerk was snoring with his head on the counter, so I eased up the well-worn flight of stairs.

On the second floor, I glanced down the dark hall to see a string of pale light along the bottom of a door. Softly I knocked on her door.

"Who is it?"

I heard the wariness in her tone. "Desk clerk. Got a message for you from some guy."

She muttered a couple curses, then jerked open the door. Her eyes bulged. I stepped inside and closed the door behind quickly.

"Sorry I was late for the welcome you had for me."

She glared at me. In the glare of the cold light of the single bulb dangling from the ceiling on her puffy face, I saw that my estimate of her being in her late thirties or early forties was indeed too generous. She was fifty if she were a day, and fifty-five wasn't too far out of the question. "You better get out of here. Jojo and Candy will be here anytime."

I ignored her threat. "You said you knew something about the fire at the Hip-Hop. Or were you lying to me?"

She studied me a moment. The defiance on her pasty face faded. She glanced at the door behind me and dragged her tongue across her lips. "You still got the hundred bucks?"

"If you give me good information."

For several moments, she pondered the offer. Finally she shook her head and, gazing everywhere except at me, replied, "I was lying to you. I don't know nothing."

I didn't believe her. "Are you afraid of what Jojo and Candy'll do if you tell me? They don't need to know."

"No. That ain't it. I just don't know nothing."

The more she protested, the more convinced I was that she knew something: a name, a piece of gossip, something that might be the break I was looking for. "I'll make it two hundred. I'll give you twenty-four hours to get a bus out of town before I act on what you tell me."

She considered the offer several moments, then shook her head again. "I can't." She dropped her gaze to the floor.

This time, she had not denied knowing anything about the fire, which told me that my hunch was right. She had information, which for whatever reason, she was afraid to reveal.

I never liked putting undue pressure on anyone, especially ones like Wanda who, for one reason or another, were caught up in the vortex of a life they couldn't escape. But, in a soft almost compassionate voice, I said, "What would happen if I spread word on the street that you were cooperating with me and the cops?"

She jerked her head up, gaping at me in disbelief. "But I ain't."

I arched an eyebrow. "I know that. You know that. But Jojo and Candy don't."

Her lips quivered. Her watery gray eyes pleaded with me. "Look, Mister. They'd hurt me bad if they thought I was stooling to the cops."

"They don't have to know. You said everyone on the street knew about it, so how would they know word came from you?"

She didn't answer.

I continued. "Was it Jojo or Candy?"

"Huh?" Her eyes widened in surprise. "No. All they wanted was the hundred bucks. All they know how to do is beat up on women."

"Why do you hang around then? Get out of here. Find a new life for yourself."

She snorted. "How?" She gestured to the bare walls of the shabby room. "I got nothing and nowhere to go."

At that moment, I knew I wasn't going to play out my bluff and spread lies about her on the street. I'd always been a sucker for a sob story. "You have any family?"

"A sister. In Denver. I ain't seen her in five years."

"Look, Wanda. Forget about the fire. I'll find out from someone else, but if you want to get out this, I'll take you to the bus station and buy you a ticket to Denver, and I'll give you the two hundred bucks if you promise not to come back to Austin."

Tears gathered in her eyes as she looked up at me in disbelief. She stammered for words. "Why—Why would you do that for me, someone you don't know?"

I grinned. I knew, but the morality ingrained in a Cajun boy from the crib up is hard to explain without sounding pompous. "Beats me. It just seems like the thing to do. How about it?"

Slowly she nodded.

I added. "Remember. One condition. Don't ever come back to Austin."

She nodded again.

At 7:00 that morning, my tail dragging from no sleep, I stood with Wanda in the boarding line of the Greyhound Bus. In addition to the two hundred bucks, I supplied her with three magazines and a small bag of snacks.

We made our way slowly to the open door without saying a word. I held her elbow as she stepped up on the first step. She took another step up, paused, and turned back to me. "Bull Abdo," she said softly. "He's who you're looking for. Bull Abdo."

Her words stunned me for a moment. Finally, I collected my thoughts. "Where can I find him?"

She shrugged helplessly. "All I know about him is that he's got a busted nose from the ring."

Chapter Sixteen

I watched the bus head down Eighth Street and turn north on I-35 for Fort Worth after which I drove straight to the office, parking in my usual spot. I sat in the truck for several moments.

Wanda's revelation of Bull Abdo and a broken nose flushed adrenaline through my veins. I sat staring blankly out the side window at the traffic on Lamar, trying to figure my first step in running down Bull Abdo.

There were three options: Danny O'Banion, Bob Ray Burrus at the police station, and S.S. at Neon Larry's. I didn't know which one was the best choice, so I decided to contact all three.

I grinned, noticing from my reflection in the window I needed a shave. A sudden yawn caught. I closed my eyes and stretched. I laid my head against the headrest for a moment.

Next thing I knew, someone was tapping on my window. I opened my eyes to see the grinning face of Doreen Patterson.

"You look terrible," she said as I climbed from the pickup.

"That's what no sleep does for you."

"What happened?"

While crossing the parking lot, I briefly sketched out the night's events after we had separated.

The rich aroma of fresh coffee filled my nostrils when we pushed through the office door. We headed directly for the coffeepot. "You think she was telling you the truth? I mean about this guy Bull Abdo."

"I'd like to think so," I replied, filling a mug with coffee. I sipped it, and the delightful heat of the coffee warmed me all the way down to the pit of my stomach. "Of course, I wouldn't be surprised if she was down at the Blue Light right now, but I'd like to think she's finally got her head together."

"Have you ever heard of this Abdo guy?"

"Nope, but a few phone calls should tell us something about him."

"Don't forget, we didn't see Abe Romero yesterday."

"We will this morning, after Towers, our crystal expert."

One inconvenience in my line of work is that I'm an early person. I've always risen early and run out of steam early. The majority of those with whom I interact are night people, and running them down in the mornings is just about as impossible as giving a cat a pill.

I dialed Danny's number. A voice with all the charm of a pet rock said he would be in at 10:00. Call back.

Neon Larry's didn't answer, which was probably just as well, for if S.S. wasn't there, whoever answered would be of no help.

And Bob Ray promised to see what he could find.

I replaced the receiver and glanced at my watch, unable to believe it was only 9:00. To my fuzzy brain and weary muscles, it was time for bed. I sighed and leaned back. Maybe I could catch a short nap.

"What about The Lighthouse and pawnshop?"

"Huh?" I frowned at Doreen. "What about them?"

"You said you wanted to drop by there before we visited Towers."

With a grimace, I closed my eyes and shook my head. "That's right. I'd forgotten all about it." Groaning, I pushed myself to my feet. "Then's let's go see Jimmy Wong and then Mrs. Bernie."

Jimmy Wong grinned amiably and his eyes lit up when he spotted me. "Ah, Tony-san. It is good to see you." He touched his slender fingers to his lips. "You and the lady wish for tea, coffee?"

I noticed a small bandage on his hand. "Either'll be fine." We slid in at a small round table.

Doreen whispered. "I'm not certain, but he looks like the one who came running in last night soaking wet."

Jimmy sat the coffee in front of us and eased into a chair. He clapped his hands together softly. "Ah, so now my friend. What is it I can do for you?"

I introduced Doreen and cut right to the chase. "Someone came in here last night soaking wet. Did you happen to see him?"

A puzzled frown replaced the friendly smile on his face. He glanced at Doreen and then back at me. "Is this important, Tonysan?"

"I'm not sure, Jimmy. Truth is, I'm just gathering information. A source mentioned he saw this person run in here."

The diminutive man's eyes laughed. "Whoever this source might be, he was right. He saw me run in. A hot water hose on my washing machine at Devil's Den broke. I soaked myself turning off the water." He held up his hand. "The hot water burned me."

During the drive to the pawnshop, Doreen chided herself. "Looks like I goofed on that."

"Not at all. Hey, that's what happens in this game. Win some, lose some. The secret is just to keep playing. Who knows," I added with a shrug, "maybe we'll score a touchdown out at the pawnshop."

Mrs. Bernie grinned when we entered her shop. Pulling the ever-present cigarette from her lips, she blew a stream of smoke into the air. "Well, you two was right. I had me a little visitor last night." She slid off the stool and gestured to the locked door beside her barred window. "Come on in here. I'll show you." She glanced at the floor. "Stay, Max."

A soft growl responded to her command.

I heard Doreen catch her breath.

A tumbler on the lock clicked, and the heavy door swung open. She chuckled. "Don't worry, folks," Mrs. Bernie said. "Max is a real gentleman until somebody he don't know comes in here at night."

I shot a hasty glance at Max as I stepped through the door.

Being unfamiliar with Rottweilers, I couldn't guess how much the huge dog weighed, but when he had hold of the tail of my jacket last night, it felt like a five-hundred-pound anvil was dangling there.

Max lay on the floor, his eyes fixed on us.

"Back here," she said, pointing down an aisle between two rows of stacked shelves.

Doreen gasped when we spotted the dried blood smeared over the concrete floor leading to the rear door.

"Cops came out this morning. Don't know why. I could of told them what happened. Whoever this guy was, he got about halfway down the aisle here before Max got him." She took a deep drag off her cigarette and added, "Tore him up some. Even tore off a piece of his coat or pants. I don't know which."

I frowned at her. "I don't suppose you have it."

With a hint of disdain, she replied, "Naw. You know how them cops are. Nothing makes them any happier than to go back to the station with some evidence." She snorted. "Makes it look like they been working or something."

She laughed, and I laughed with her.

Doreen spoke up. "What color was the patch?" She glanced at me. I was thinking the same thing.

Mrs. Bernie shrugged. "Blue."

"With stripes?" Doreen asked.

The older woman frowned. "I—I don't remember seeing none. Maybe."

Nodding slowly, I glanced up and down the shelves that stretched to the ceiling, each bulging with various items. "Is anything missing?"

She grinned, revealing tobacco-stained teeth. "You mean the skull?"

"Yeah."

"Nope. Still there. Still waiting until October fifteen."

I studied her a moment. "Mrs. Bernie, can I ask a favor?"

Her forehead knit in a frown. She glanced at Doreen, then replied, "Depends."

"You remember I told you the old wino who pawned the skull was dead. Someone murdered him. I think the killer was after that skull. If he'd found the ticket, he would have already redeemed the skull. If someone comes in with the ticket, will you call me?" I handed her a card.

She studied the card a moment. "What about the cops?"

"They've already closed the case. They figure the old wino set the fire and hit his head when he was trying to run away."

I could see her wheels turning in her head. "Who was the old man to you?"

With a shrug, I replied, "Just someone I knew. He never hurt anybody in the world except himself."

Slowly, she nodded. "All right. I'll give you a call."

"It's the same guy," Doreen exclaimed when we climbed in the Silverado. "It has to be." Energized by Mrs. Bernie's reply, she added, "Do you think it was that Bull Abdo?"

I shrugged and pulled onto the bridge over the river, heading for Towers' Jewelry. "Looks more and more like it might be. But remember, she wasn't sure about the material." The newest discovery had me keyed up despite a lack of sleep. "And of course, there are a thousand blue pinstriped suits out there."

She looked around at me. Arching an eyebrow. "Maybe, but stop and think. Who is usually wearing them? Now you might think I'm crazy, but I can think of two types of men who wear them regularly, and one of them is not the average guy on the street. My ex wore suits all the time. He had a pinstripe, but he never wore it unless he was meeting with upper-level management and CEOs. That's the first type. I knocked around a few years doing clerical work, so I know. Your bigwigs, the real big ones, wear pinstripes. It's a power thing, like solid red ties."

For a few moments, I considered her observation. "You said two. What other group wears them?"

Doreen hesitated.

"Well?"

"It sounds silly."

"So? I promise I won't laugh."

She chuckled. "The guy who slammed you into the wall and ran into the Red Rabbit wore a blue pinstripe suit."

"Okay. And?"

"So, Mister Detective, did you pay any attention to the suits O'Banion's boys wore?" Without giving me a chance to reply, she continued, "The first one, the one I thought was a parking lot boy—remember him? Well, he wore pinstripes, blue if I remember right. And the big guy, the vegetarian—"

"Huey."

"Yeah. He wore a gray pinstripe." She paused and cleared her throat. "I don't know why, or even if it's true, but it seems a certain element on the wrong side of the law prefers pinstripes."

I frowned at her suggestion. "In other words, you think we're looking for either goombahs or business executives?"

She smiled. "I said you'd laugh."

"Not me." I shook my head. "I learned long ago never to discount any idea regardless of how much it pushes the envelope."

I've often heard it said that life is stranger than fiction. I learned the hard way never to argue with that little maxim. For all I knew, Bull Abdo could very well be the one for whom we were searching.

Doreen whistled when we pulled into the parking lot of Towers' Jewelry. The block–long, two-story building had a Spanish facade of white stucco walls with a red-tiled roof. The portico was supported with graceful, fifteen-foot arches, revealing the office windows on the second floor.

"We should have brought my Jag," she muttered, eyeing the BMWs, Mercedes, and Lexus parked in the lot. There was even a Rolls. She eyed the interior of my pickup with a critical eye. She arched an eyebrow. "They might not even let you park here."

I grinned back. "No? Let's see them stop me," I replied, pulling into a vacant spot between a Jaguar and Lexus in front of the main door. I shifted into park and looked at her. "Tell me. What is it you don't like about pickups?"

The smile fled her face and for a moment, her black eyes blazed fire. Slowly, she relaxed and a faint smile curled the frown from her lips. "My ex drove pickups. As long as I can remember, he drove them. When I left him, I swore I'd never ride in one of these—" She paused, searching for the right word.

"Stinking?"

Her smile grew wider. "Yes. Stinking's a good word. I swore I'd never ride in one of these stinking things again." She paused, then added, "Present company excepted."

I grinned at her.

At that moment, two tastefully attired women wearing heels, expensive dresses, and funny little hats emerged from the front door and jerked to a surprised halt, staring at the white hood of my Chevy pickup.

Reaching for the door handle, I ignored them, and then my cell rang. I answered it. "Boudreaux."

"It's me, Tony—Bob Ray. I got your stuff about Abdo. I don't know what you're going to do with it, but I got it."

Chapter Seventeen

"Carlos Abdo, aka The Bull, is a low-level hood with a rap sheet as long as your leg. It's the usual stuff: breaking and entering, car theft, dealing. He just got out of Huntsville a couple months back. Right now, he's on parole. According to his parole officer, he's been a good little boy. Never misses an appointment, pays his fees on time, and stays away from the wine, women, and song. Currently, he's working for Moran's Laundry, picking up and delivering."

"His boss knows he's an ex-con?"

"Naturally. Parole officer got him the job. Boss is pleased with Abdo's work."

"Thanks, Bob Ray. You're a lifesaver." I jotted the information on one of my ubiquitous cards and slid it in my pocket. Now, to finish up my little file of Carlos

Abdo, all I had to do was touch base with Danny and S.S. and see what they could tell me about the guy.

J. C. Towers was a slight, diminutive man, fitting the exact image I had of a jeweler.

Dressed immaculately in a black pinstripe suit, which Doreen furtively pointed out to me with a gleeful grin, Towers rose from behind an ornately carved desk and, in a soft, well-modulated voice, greeted us. "Mister Boudreaux. A pleasure to meet you. Any friend of Beatrice Morrison is more than welcome to Towers' Jewels. We are quite proud of the integrity we at Towers display in dealing with all of our customers." He looked at Doreen and waited, an expectant smile on his slender face.

The cynic in me couldn't help wondering whom he was trying to convince about the quality of the company's integrity, us or himself. "Same here, Mister Towers. This is my—" I hesitated. I started to introduce Doreen as my partner, but the word would have probably been too crass for such a classy joint. Instead, I introduced her as, "My associate, Ms. Patterson."

He nodded briefly to her, then gestured to the chairs in front of his desk. "Now, what can I do for you?" he asked as he sat behind the desk. His face wore an expression best described as pained tolerance.

"Beatrice, that is, Mrs. Morrison said you were an expert on crystal. Ms. Patterson and I are trying to find someone who is an expert on crystal skulls."

If you've ever built a sand castle on the beach and poured water over it, you remember how quickly it melts. That was how quickly the expression on his face melted into astonishment. My question must have shaken his composure for he stammered, "I beg your pardon?"

"Crystal skulls, Mister Towers. We're looking for an expert on crystal skulls."

He nodded slowly and leaned back in his chair, steepling his fingers on his thin chest. "Are you familiar with them, Mister Boudreaux?" A crafty gleam sharpened his eyes like the cut of a fine diamond.

"Only what I found online, that there are a half-dozen or so skulls considered ancient, carved by techniques not even in existence until the last few decades."

He nodded and leaned forward, a calculating glitter coming to life in his eyes. "There are many more than half-a-dozen crystal skulls, Mister Boudreaux, but you are correct in that those six or so are the only ones considered ancient."

I frowned, not wanting to believe our good luck. "You—You know about crystal skulls?"

He gestured to his office. "I possess none, but in my area of expertise, I hear much of them, and I might add, the stories are fascinating."

"So, you know about them?"

He shrugged. "Some."

Doreen and I grinned at each other. "Are those things real?"

"The skulls? Oh, yes! Remarkable—I might say impossible creations—but they exist."

"What can you tell us about them? Say, the Nelson-Vines skull."

His eyes popped open like a stepped-on toad frog, but he quickly regained his composure. "Nelson-Vines, you say." I nodded, and he continued. "She—I mean, the Nelson-Vines is probably the most well known of all the crystal skulls. The skull is of clear quartz crystal from the same rock. Because of the size, it is generally considered that of a woman. That's why the skull is often referred to as *she*."

"Have you ever seen it?"

"Once, at an exhibit at the Santa Clara Museum in California. Several startling features about the skull add to its mysticism."

I leaned forward. "Such as . . ."

"First, the skull was carved against the natural axis of the crystal." When I frowned, he explained, "Sculptors always take into account the axis, the orientation of the crystal's molecular symmetry. If they carve against the grain, the piece is bound to shatter even with the use of lasers and other high-tech methods."

About all I really understood was "carving against the grain." "But that's how this skull was cut, huh? Against the grain."

"Yes."

"What kind of explanation is there for it?"

A faint smile curled his lips. "None." Before I could

reply, he continued, "In addition to that conundrum, researchers, using state-of-the-art optics, could find no microscopic scratches on the crystal to indicate it had been carved with metal instruments."

I glanced at Doreen, unsure if Towers was telling us the truth or just having fun with us.

He must have spotted the skeptical expression on my face for nodded and said, "I felt the same way, Mister Boudreaux. To add still more mythic enigma to the aura of the Nelson-Vines, Doctor Samuel Borland of the California Lapidary Center, the foremost expert in the world in this field, stated the skull's construction was carved with diamonds and the smoothing of the skull was accomplished by a mixture of silicon sand and water."

Nodding slowly, I leaned back, marveling at the story and expecting it was over.

There was more.

Towers arched an eyebrow. "The only problem with smoothing the skull in such a manner is that Borland estimates the man-hours involved in the process would add up to over three hundred years."

It was my turn to look like the stepped-on toad frog.

He nodded at the disbelief on my face. "As one British researcher said, 'the blasted thing shouldn't be.' "

Doreen whispered, "Tony, do you think—"

"I don't know." I looked at her helplessly.

The small man looked at us curiously. With a hint of eagerness, he said, "I have a feeling there is something you haven't told me."

Ignoring his observation, I asked, "You say there are others? Are any of them like the Nelson-Vines with the moveable jaw?"

The puzzled frown on his face deepened. "No."

Doreen's eyes grew wide.

"And this skull, the Nelson-Vines, is pretty valuable, would you say?"

"Certainly, certainly. I've been told the Nelson family has rejected offers of up to five million from various collectors around the world."

"Collectors? You mean there are people who collect these skulls?" After I made the remark, I realized just how inane it must have sounded. People collect everything.

"Certainly," he replied with a tone that seemed to suggest that only a dimwitted cretin would ask such a question.

"Who are some of these collectors? Do you remember?"

"By all means. There is Carl B. Simmons in Dallas, George Bernard of Denver, and Rosalind Attenborough of London. Those are the big three." He paused and leaned forward. "What is this all about, Mister Boudreaux? I've given you much of my time, which is quite valuable. I am entitled to an explanation."

I shook my head and leaned back in the plush leather chair. "Give me a second. I'm trying to sort my thoughts here."

Doreen took over. "Mister Towers. If the Nelson-Vines skull turned up missing, would you have heard about it?"

He looked at her. "Most certainly. In the field of crystal skulls, word travels fast. Is it?"

"We're asking you."

"Look, Mister Towers," I said. "Here's the situation. We found a glass skull, a small one, with a movable jaw. It looks like the skull might be the reason for a murder. We need someone to take a look at this skull and tell us if it is valuable or just a piece of glass. Can you do that?"

His eyes glittered with excitement. "You have one, a crystal skull?"

"No, but we know where it is."

He rubbed his hands together. "Certainly I'll look at it. When can you get it to me?"

I chuckled and Doreen replied. "You'll have to go with us. The current owner won't let it out of her sight."

After a moment, he agreed.

I punched in Mrs. Bernie's number and asked if she minded if I brought someone to look at the skull.

"Nope, don't mind a bit, but it ain't getting out of my sight. I got my .357 and Max, don't forget."

I chuckled. "I could never forget Max."

After I hung up, Towers frowned. "Who's Max?"

Doreen laughed. "You'll see."

Towers hesitated when he saw my pickup. He pointed a manicured finger. "This? The three of us?"

I laughed. "We're all skinny. We'll fit in front."

During the ride to Bernie's, Towers revealed more of the lore of the ancient skulls. "There is a British crystal skull and a Paris skull. The specimen in Paris is called the Aztec Skull. The British skull is on display in the British Museum of Man in London. The Aztec Skull was on display at the Trocadero Museum, but a few years ago, it was taken off display."

"Why was that?" I flexed my fingers about the wheel and clicked on my left-turn signal.

He grew solemn. "It kept moving."

I glanced at him, expecting a smile. His thin face remained somber.

Doreen asked. "What do you mean, moving?"

"The Aztec Skull was displayed in a locked case. One morning the curator noticed the skull was not on its stand, but was in another section of the display case. He placed it back on its stand and instructed the docents not to handle the skull again. Naturally, they all protested their innocence, so he changed locks on the case and kept the only key in his possession. To his astonishment, the next morning, the skull had moved off the stand to another corner of the case."

Doreen grunted. "Someone's idea of a joke."

Towers shook his head. Somberly, he replied, "No. The skull was placed under twenty-four-hour surveillance."

I glanced at him. "And?"

He arched an eyebrow. "The camera recorded the

movement. A force, whatever it was, slowly moved the skull to the far end of the display case."

Doreen frowned. "How is such a thing possible?"

A faint smile played over his thin lips. "It isn't, but it happened, just like the Nelson-Vines skull is impossible. Consequently, the museum administrator took the skull off display."

I whistled softly. "That I would have to see to believe."

We parked in front of Bernie's Pawnshop, and Towers finished his account of the skulls. "The Aztec Skull was believed carved by either the ancient Mayans or Aztecs for religious purposes. There are many believers in the world today who insist the skull possesses a supernatural mysticism and that it is linked to sacred world prophecies once held by those vanished cultures."

While I was having a difficult time believing what I was hearing, I had seen enough inexplicable events in my forty-odd years to convince me that as soon as you thought you'd seen everything, you would witness an event beyond belief.

Who was to say this wasn't one of them?

Chapter Eighteen

Towers almost fainted when he saw Max. "Don't worry, Mister," Mrs. Bernie laughed and pulled a Kleenex from the pocket of the tattered sweater she wore over her baggy purple print dress. "Max is a real gentleman until I tell him otherwise." She gestured down one aisle. "This way."

Halfway down, she stopped and pulled the crystal skull off the shelf. "Here it is." She stuck it in Towers' hands.

He nodded tersely and turned on his heel. The ominous click of the .357 stopped him.

"Where do you think you're going, mister?"

His face blanched. "I—ah, what I mean is—the light here is bad. I—I just want to get to a window, that's all."

"Oh. That's all right. Go ahead."

He gulped hard two or three times as he headed for

the window where he retrieved his loupe from his vest pocket and fit it to his eye.

After studying the skull for a few minutes, he looked around. "The quartz is too smoky to be the Nelson-Vines, but from what I can ascertain from such a hasty inspection—" He glanced uncomfortably at Mrs. Bernie. "It is almost a duplicate of the Nelson-Vines."

He handed it back to Mrs. Bernie. "Madam, I would be most interested in purchasing this item from you." He glanced uneasily at me, then continued, "To be perfectly honest, it is a rare find."

I noticed he did not put a price on the "rare find."

Mrs. Bernie looked up at me. "How much do you think the skull is worth, Boudreaux?"

Towers' eyes pleaded with me not to reveal the figure he had earlier quoted. So much for his integrity.

"I don't know for sure, but earlier, Mister Towers mentioned that the owners of a similar skull turned down a five million dollar offer."

Towers' face crumbled as Mrs. Bernie stared at me in disbelief. Her eyes grew suspicious. "What is this, some kind of joke?"

Doreen spoke up. "No, Mrs. Bernie. That's what he said."

I took up where Doreen left off. "If that's the case, Mrs. Bernie, then you need to put that skull somewhere safe, real safe."

The indifferent expression on her face told me she didn't believe me. She gestured to Max. "It's safe here."

"Think about it, Mrs. Bernie. These guys are serious. If they'd known Max was here, he'd be dead now. Next time they come back, they'll take him out. Maybe you. They've killed one already. Another won't make any difference."

A few knots of concern wrinkled her forehead. "You think?"

Doreen stepped forward and laid her hand on the older woman's arm. "Yes."

The older woman turned back to me. "What should I do?"

I glanced at J. C. Towers, and an idea hit me.

"Now, you can do what you want, Mrs. Bernie, but Mister Towers is an expert plus his business has a safe impossible to break into. He would probably be willing to keep it in his safe for you until it defaults with the understanding that you two would be partners in whatever arrangement he can make to sell the skull."

At first, Towers stared at me in disbelief, but then a slow smile played over his lips as he understood the terms of the arrangement. He knew he could never solely possess the skull, so applying the common sense approach to business that fifty percent of something is better than a hundred percent of nothing, he agreed.

Mrs. Bernie eyed the diminutive man skeptically. "What about it? If the skull is defaulted, can you find a buyer for it?"

He rubbed his hands together. "Certainly, certainly."

She narrowed her eyes. "Come with me." She turned on her heel and led us from the storage room and stopped in front of the barred window that she sat behind. She turned to him. "Eighty-twenty is the only way I'd go. Me with the eighty."

The diminutive man stiffened, then studied her with a calculating eye. "Madam," he began in a haughty tone, "I possess the contacts for the most advantageous transaction. I would think at least a fifty-fifty agreement most appropriate."

Mrs. Bernie hesitated a moment. "Seventy-thirty."

Towers pursed his lips. "Sixty-forty."

She nodded abruptly and took the skull from him and slipped it under her arm like a football. She retrieved a battered pack of Pall Mall cigarettes from her sweater pocket and lit one as J. C. Towers looked on in horror at her casual treatment of the skull. She inhaled and blew the smoke into the air. As it drifted to the ceiling, she stuck her face in Towers'. "No hanky panky, no rich guy moves to keep the skull? Otherwise, I'll sic Max on you. Okay?"

A flicker of irritation knit the small man's brows, but he quickly recovered. "My word, Madam."

"These two here are our witnesses, Doreen Patterson and Tony Boudreaux. Is that all right with you, Mister Towers?"

He nodded. "Yes."

"And you are the J. C. Towers who owns Tower Jewelers?"

"Yes."

"Here in Austin, Texas?"

Towers frowned at me momentarily. I cut my eyes toward Doreen. She was just as puzzled as I was by Mrs. Bernie's behavior as well as her last few questions. A ludicrous thought crossed my mind. Were we witnessing an early stage of senility in the old lady?

She studied him another moment. Without taking her eyes off him, she said, "What do you think, Max?"

Max barked once.

J. C. Towers took a step back.

"Don't worry, Mister Towers," she said with a chuckle. "Max thinks you're okay." He started to smile until she added. "I ain't sure, but Max ain't been fooled in the last ten years." She pointed to a camera in the ceiling. "I make it a habit to make a record of everyone who comes to my window. Had to use it a few times. Kind of expensive, but it's tax deductible. Move around to your left some, Mister Towers. I want the camera of get a clear shot when I give you the skull."

So much for senility.

Towers stammered but did as she asked.

She held out the skull. He reached for it, but she held tightly. "One more thing," she said.

"Whatever you say, Madam," Towers croaked.

"I want to watch you put it in your safe."

He nodded eagerly. "As you say, Mrs. Bernie. As you say."

But, that was to prove a problem. While Mrs. Bernie secured the fortress-like walls of the business, she informed us that she did not drive. "Mister Bernie drove me everywhere. I never learned to drive. Red Cap Taxi picks me up and drops me off." She paused before locking the door to the storeroom. "Don't worry, Max. I'll be back in thirty minutes."

She peered out the window. "The pickup yours?"

"Yeah."

She grinned. "Crowded, but it'll work."

Towers sputtered. "You mean, we—" He gestured to us. "The four of us are going to ride in that?"

Mrs. Bernie laughed and slapped him on the shoulder. "Sure Mister Towers. No trouble. Mister Bernie and me have musta rode four or five in a pickup a thousand times."

"But, but—"

She eyed his slender frame and then her substantial build. "I was going to say I'd sit in your lap, but I think you best sit on mine."

As we pulled out of the parking lot onto Congress Avenue, I glanced in the side mirror and spotted a yellow Jeep with black fenders and three black lightning bolts on the side exit a parking lot on the opposite side of the street and fall in behind by several car lengths. I didn't think too much about it until I looked back again and spotted it still behind us.

I kept my speed below the limit, so naturally vehicles swept past us on the left and right. All except the Jeep.

We must have been a curious sight heading across the Congress Avenue Bridge all scrunched in the cab of my Silverado. Mister Towers had to hunker over just to see out the front window.

The trip didn't take any longer than five minutes. While waiting to turn left into Towers' Jewels from the turning lane, I noticed the Jeep take a right into downtown. I grinned to myself. My imagination had been working overtime.

I couldn't help grinning at just how stunned Towers' upscale customers were when they spotted us piling out of the pickup and pushing through the door of the jewelry store. More than just a few eyes grew wide and a few mouths dropped open as the diminutive man scurried across the carpeted floor to his office, followed by an anomalous group including a ponderous woman wearing a purple print dress and tattered sweater and dangling a half-smoked Pall Mall from her lips; a tall woman wearing little makeup and a brown business suit; and a PI in washed-out jeans, tweed jacket, and wearing a sappy grin on his face.

Five minutes later, the three of us climbed back in my pickup. I looked over at Mrs. Bernie. "Satisfied?"

She grinned warmly. "Ain't you?"

Doreen laughed. "Yes."

I started the engine and backed out. At that moment, a yellow-and-black Jeep with three black lightning bolts on the side drove past, heading south back across the Congress Avenue Bridge. I arched an eyebrow. Maybe my imagination wasn't working overtime after all.

Chapter Nineteen

After we dropped Mrs. Bernie at her shop, we stopped in a local deli for a light lunch. We must have looked like overage college kids sitting there, scribbling out our notes between bites of chicken salad and gulps of tea.

Glancing under my eyebrows at Doreen, I had to admit that despite that first day or so, we were beginning to work together. I don't know if it were that little talk we had the second day or what. All I know is that life is so much less complicated when people try to get along with those around them.

Next thing I knew, my head was bobbing and someone was shaking my shoulder. "Wake up."

"Huh!" I jerked awake.

Doreen was grinning at me. "Tell you what. After

lunch, let's pick up my car. You can nap on the way out to Texas Star in Elgin."

For a moment, I stared at her. "Texas Star?" Somewhere in my weary and fuzzy brain, the words struck a familiar chord, but for the life of me, I couldn't place the tune.

"Abe Romero! Remember him?"

I closed my eyes and leaned back. "Sorry. I guess I'm more tired than I thought." I pushed to my feet. "Be right back."

In the Men's Room, I splashed water on my face and dried it with a paper towel. The effort helped, but not enough for me to refuse her offer to drive us.

When I woke up staring at the front of the Texas Star, head throbbing, mouth dry, and my eyes burning, I felt worse than when I went to sleep. I groaned.

Doreen chirped. "Feel better?"

"No." I grunted, blinking against the bright sunlight and still groggy with sleep. I fumbled to open the door, but I couldn't find the handle.

Doreen leaned over and opened the door. "Here."

I don't think I could ever own a sports car, primarily because I couldn't get use to looking between my knees every time I swung my legs around and planted my feet on the ground to get out of the vehicle.

Cavernous as a competition-sized gym, the dimly illumined interior of Texas Star was a welcome respite to the glare of the September sun. The portly bartender grinned when he spotted me. "Hey, Tony. How's the man? Where you been keeping yourself?"

Doreen glanced at me curiously, but I paid her no attention. "Hey, Big Tim." I slid up on a stool at the bar. Doreen did the same. "Give me a cup of coffee, Timmy. I'm dragging." I glanced at Doreen. "You want anything?"

Her face a mask of ice, she snapped, "No. Nothing."

I frowned at the chill in her voice for a moment, then dismissed it, too tired to worry about her change in mood.

"Here you go, Tony." Wearing his perpetual grin, Big Tim slid a steaming mug of coffee in front of me. "What's up? Slumming?"

I gulped the hot black liquid and suppressed a grimace at its lack of strength. Of course, I'd rather have had a beer, but then I would have had a guilty conscience. Oh yeah, I backslid from time to time, but despite my transgressions in the time I'd been with AA, I felt fairly well-satisfied with the curb I'd put on my drinking.

I introduced Doreen. "We're looking for a guy named Abe Romero. Danny said he'd been hanging out around here."

Big Tim's grin grew wider. "Abe? Sure. He's the dude in the fancy duds over there shooting pool. So, how's Danny? I ain't seen him in couple months."

"Danny's good. We had dinner with him Monday night."

"Yeah," Big Tim exclaimed. "And I bet I can tell you where. County Line Barbecue." He grinned at Doreen and in an effort to be friendly, said, "Right, Doreen?"

Her face remained frozen. "Right," was all she said.

I glanced at her, puzzled by her sudden hostility.

For a moment, the grin on Big Tim's lips flickered and he turned back to me, the expression in his eyes and on his face asking me what was wrong with her. He forced a laugh. "Yep. That's always where he goes. When they plant that one, they'll have to put a plate of barbecue in the coffin with him."

I slid off the stool and headed for the pool tables in the rear of the cavernous room. "Take it easy, Big Tim," I said.

"Yeah. You too, Tony." He hesitated, then added, "Doreen."

Abe Romero was about three inches taller than me, and a third again as wide. I guessed his weight at about two-thirty or two-forty. He looked in good shape and the expensive suit he wore fit him perfectly. I had feeling it was custom made.

We stopped several feet from the table while his opponent lined up the cue ball on a stripe and missed. Romero laughed and promptly sank the last two solids and then the eight ball. He straightened and laid his cue stick on the green felt. "That's another one, Mule. Two fifty."

I stepped forward. "Romero? Abe Romero?"

He looked around at us with a frown. "Yeah? You want a game?"

"No. My name is Tony Boudreaux, and this is Doreen Patterson. We're investigating the fire of a business you wanted to buy down on Sixth Street."

His frown deepened a moment, then he nodded. "You talking 'bout the Hip-Hop?"

"Yeah. Got a minute?"

His eyes narrowed suspiciously. "You cops?"

"No. Private Investigators working for Getdown Joe Sillery. You know Joe."

"Yeah. I know Joe. So why talk to me? I didn't have nothing to do with the fire. Hey, I wanted to buy the place."

"That's what Getdown told us. We're just talking to everyone who was connected to the place. You know, see if you had any idea who might have had a grudge against Getdown."

He curled one side of his lips in a sneer. "There's plenty who got grudges against the fat man."

I pulled out a pen and note card. From the corner of my eye, I saw Doreen do the same. "Such as?"

Romero pursed his lips. "Let's see, there's Clay Renfield. Getdown fired him from managing the place after six years. Ticked Clay off something fierce. And then there was old Rocket."

Frowning across the table at Romero, I said. "Rocket?"

"Yeah. Ralph Sloane. Getdown Joe reneged on selling

Rocket a piece of the action. Rocket talked to his mouth-piece about suing the fat man."

Doreen broke into the conversation. "Breach of promise?"

Romero frowned at her. "Huh?"

"A contract. Was a contract broken?"

"Naw. Just talk between them, but I heard it. I heard Getdown tell Rocket he'd sell for a hundred yards."

Doreen's pen paused in mid-air. She looked up from her notes. "Yard."

"Thousand," I explained. "A hundred thousand."

"Yeah," Romero continued. "I figured the fat man was nuts for backing off. He could have used the bread."

"Oh?" I arched an eyebrow.

Romero nodded. "That's what I said. Word on the street was Joe was hurting. The hundred thou' would have pulled him out of the heat, at least for a couple weeks."

The revelation smacked me between the eyes. Before I could stammer out my response, Doreen did it for us. "But from what he said, the Hip-Hop was like the federal mint."

With a soft chuckle, Romero nodded. "It is." He paused and held up a finger over his head. "Yo! Timmy!" He glanced at us. "Beer? Wine?"

I shook my head. "No. So, why did he need the cash?"

"The fat guy is a big spender, vacations, ski lodges, all that sort of thing. He gets his kicks from rubbing shoulders with them high-profile rappers and actors. From what I heard, he was trying to bankroll a nation-wide concert tour for some of the big rap groups, and he come up short."

For the life of me, I couldn't imagine roly-poly Get-down Joe on skis—snow, or water. "If he needed cash that much, why would he back out of a deal with Sloane?" I shook my head and looked at Doreen. "That doesn't make sense."

She remained silent, eyeing me coldly.

Now, I've had more than my share of problems with the fairer gender, having been married and divorced years back. Fortunately, we had no offspring, and the divorce was amicable. I walked away with my clothing and an aquarium of exotic fish, one named Oscar who suffered brain damage when an old teaching buddy and stand-up comic got drunk one night and mistook the aquarium for the john.

So, from the chilly vibes emanating from her slender body in every direction just like the spines on a porcu-pine, I knew something had put the proverbial burr un-der her saddle.

"That's what I thought," Romero replied as Big Tim sat a can of Budweiser on the edge of the pool table. He sipped the beer and dragged the back of his hand across his lips. "Sure you won't have one?"

"Positive. You think Sloane was ticked off enough to torch the place?"

He pursed his lips a moment, then shook his head. "Naw. He bought him another place out on South Thirty-Five a couple miles on the other side of Ben White Boulevard. Probably not Renfield either. From what I heard, he went to work for Buck Topper a couple doors away."

"He the one covered with tattoos?"

Abe nodded. "Yeah. Know him?"

"Saw him. One more question. Why did you want to buy the Hip-Hop?"

A sly smile played over his lips. He straightened the knot of his pale-pink tie in the center of the light-blue collar. "Truth is, I make my large by buying goods at rock-bottom prices and selling high. I knew Joe was hard up for cash, so I thought I take a flier. If I could steal the Hip-Hop, I coulda turned a nice profit."

Pursing my lips, I nodded. "How much did you offer?"

He lifted an eyebrow. "That's kinda personal."

I chuckled. "I agree."

He shrugged. "What the heck. A hundred thousand."

"The same as Sloane?" Doreen asked suspiciously.

"Why not? Joe might have been having second thoughts. I've seen that happen dozens of times. Some old boy turns down an offer, then cusses hisself later." He paused, grinned. "But, that wasn't one of those times."

Slipping my cards back in my pocket, I thanked him. He'd given us more to chew on. I just hoped we would find some substance in it.

After sliding into the passenger's seat of the Jaguar and buckling myself in, I looked at Doreen. "Okay. What's the problem?"

She glared at me. "Nothing, except you lied to me."

Chapter Twenty

For a moment, I gaped at her, unable to believe I was suddenly back into a world of eggshells. "What are you talking about?"

She jabbed an unpainted fingernail at the Texas Star. "Yesterday morning, you told me to find the address of this place. You already knew it." Her eyes narrowed. "What's going on here?"

My fevered brain raced, trying to make some sense of what she was saying. Then I remembered when Marty had called me into his office. Because I was ready to spill my dislike and reservations about Doreen, I didn't want her with us, so I had indeed given her some busy work, although I wouldn't exactly call it a lie. A deception, okay; but, I'd like to beg off on calling it a lie.

I studied her a moment. Suppressing my own anger,

I drew a deep breath. "All right. You want the truth, here it is. After that first day, Monday, I didn't want to work with you. You were hostile and antagonistic. I get enough of that from our clients. I don't need that bull from those I work with. I don't have to put up with it," I added firmly. "And I won't."

She started to reply, and I held up my hand. In a calm, and what I hoped was unthreatening tone, I continued, "Let me finish, and then you can say what you want. I had spoken with Texas Investigations on Monday—I told you about that. Well, I was going to insist Marty assign you to someone else, and the truth is, I didn't have the guts to tell him that in front of you. I asked him why you were so hostile, and that's when he told me about some of your—" I hesitated. "Well, you know, problems with your ex-husband and all." I paused. "So, I figured why not give it another chance? Obviously, I was wrong."

She studied me several moments without saying a word.

"So," I said, "there you have it. The last couple days, we've done a good job together, but it's your call. And if you don't want to keep working on this case with me, then just tell your brother-in-law. I'm quite sure your sister will help him find you another spot." I cringed at my last remark, which was hitting below the belt.

Tears formed in the corners of her eyes. "That isn't fair," she said.

I shook my head at my own insensitiveness. "I know, and I'm sorry about the sister crack." I drew a deep breath and unbuckled my seat belt. I opened the door. "I'll get a cab back."

When I started to climb out, she whispered, "No. I'll drive us back to the office."

After I closed the door, Doreen sat motionless, her fingers gripping the wheel, her eyes fixed forward. "Look. I overreacted." She looked around at me. "Sure, I know I can be a shrew. Over the years, it was just easier being that way than laying open my feelings only to have them kicked around."

She started the engine and pulled out of the parking lot. "I'll ask Marty to find another spot for me."

I wanted to shout with glee, but suddenly, I felt as if I'd done something very wrong, and I couldn't figure out just what it was.

We rode in silence for several minutes, a sense of guilt building in me. Okay, so the first day was a disaster, but the last day and a half we had worked well together, and she was a quick study, for on a couple occasions she had come up with a perceptive observation or question that had evaded me. And who could blame her for thinking I had lied. Call it anything you want, but a deception is a deception and a deception is still a lie.

When or how I made up my mind, I don't know. All I know is that just before we reached the cutoff to I-35, I glanced at her. "Where are you taking us?"

Without looking at me, she removed one finger from the wheel and pointed down the road. "To the office."

A crooked grin played over my face. "Well, before

we do that, why don't we stop by Neon Larry's on Sixth Street? See what S.S. knows about Bull Abdo."

Doreen looked around in disbelief.

I arched an eyebrow. "If you want."

A grin popped on her face, and she slashed across three lanes of traffic to hit I-35 South to downtown.

As usual, Interstate traffic was horrible, slowing us to little more than a crawl.

While we crawled along, I called Danny. He was still out. That left S.S.

We got lucky and found a parking spot half a block down from Neon Larry's. Our luck soured in Larry's for S.S. had the night off, and finding him on his night off was like chasing the proverbial will-of-the-wisp of the Louisiana swamps or the blue flame of Transylvania.

Over the years, I've always observed that there is one inevitable, one certainty, one absolute about luck. Simply, it always changes, and as Doreen and I headed back to her Jag, once again that postulation proved true for we ran across Goofyfoot and Pookie squatting in the darkened doorway of a closed bar like two bundles of grungy clothes thrown out for the garbage truck.

Naturally I gave them five bucks each, and to my surprise, Doreen handed each another five. Those two old men must have figured they had somehow stumbled through the Pearly Gates while St. Peter had his back turned.

From them we learned that Bull Abdo had been fre-
quenting the street, spending money with abandon.

"Just last night, he set up drinks for the house over to
Garcia's," Pookie said.

Goofyfoot nodded agreement. "He's been spending
like that the last week. Why, just a couple days ago, he
bought one of them fancy foreign cars like that red one
down there." He pointed to Doreen's Jag. "I suppose
he's got hisself a good job."

Pookie snorted. "Naw, he's got to be dealing or
something. Ain't no job pays like that."

Doreen and I exchanged hopeful looks. "That's in-
teresting," I replied. "Seen him around today?"

"Nope," mumbled Goofyfoot, carefully folding the
two fivers over and over into a tiny packet about an inch
square then depositing it somewhere in that volumi-
nous bundle of mismatched clothing draped over his
thin frame.

"What does he look like?"

Pookie looked up at me blankly, but I knew that expression was simply a mask.

I nodded to his heavy coat. "You got ten bucks. No
more."

A grin broke across his grimy face. "Can't blame a
guy for trying."

"So?"

"Couple inches taller than you. Hair in a ponytail,
and he's got a busted nose."

Doreen grinned at me.

"Yeah," Goofyfoot put in. "Story is he was in the ring. That's where he picked up the busted bazoo."

Doreen leaned toward me. "It's after three. You want to wait for Abdo to get off work at the laundry?"

The idea had not occurred to me. I shrugged. Why not?

We picked up a couple bottles of water and parked across in the shade of some live oaks across the street from the laundry parking lot a few minutes before five. A red Miata roadster, five or six years old, sat on one side of the lot.

"That must be Abdo's," I muttered.

Doreen put the top down. The day was one of those perfect autumn days, a brittle blue sky, an almost imperceptible nip in the air that gives you the feeling that all is right with the world.

But it wasn't.

Chapter Twenty-one

A few minutes before 5:30, the evening shift arrived. Five minutes later, the day shift began its exodus, but Carlos "the Bull" Abdo failed to appear.

We waited another thirty minutes. The Miata still remained.

"Now what?" She glanced at me.

"Stay here. I'll see what's going on."

Using the pretext of a friend who was to meet Abdo after work, I spoke with a supervisor who informed me that Abdo was at St. Mary's Hospital getting a finger set after breaking it on the job.

I jerked to a surprised halt when I left the building. There across the street, standing beside the Jag and talking to Doreen was Carlos Abdo, ponytail, flat nose, and a bandaged forefinger.

174

As I approached, Doreen smiled. "Tony, this is Carlos Abdo. We've been talking about the fire at the Hip-Hop."

His left arm was in a sling, and he was wearing a short-sleeve sport shirt. There was no sign he'd had a run-in with Max.

He nodded. "From what Ms. Patterson here says, you guys are trying to find who torched the Hip-Hop?"

Remembering Wanda's comment from early that morning that word on the street connected Abdo with the fire, I was taken aback by his casual reference to the fire. He was no moron, so I guessed he was buoyed by an ego filled with confidence. "Yeah. I was told you might be able to help us."

He arched an eyebrow. "Who told you that?"

I shrugged. "You know how it is on the street." I glanced at Doreen. "You remember where we heard it?"

With a sly gleam in her eyes, she pursed her lips and shook her head. "Around. That's all I can remember."

He grunted. In an off-hand manner, he replied, "No matter. All I know about the place is that Monday, the day before the fire, I dropped off a regular order of towels and tablecloths." He hesitated. "Oh, yeah. Getdown ordered a bunch of fancy uniforms for his people, green and yellow. We got them ready a week early, and I went ahead and delivered them too."

Somewhere in the back of my head, the words green and yellow rang a bell, but try as I might to grasp the thought, it slipped through the clumsy fingers of my mind like water.

Abdo continued. "Then I picked up all the dirty laundry. Normally, I deliver on Sixth Street twice a week, Tuesdays and Fridays, but that week, I delivered on Monday because the boilers at the laundry were going to be replaced the next day. Another reason I remember that Monday is because I ran into that old bum that got hisself killed in the fire." He grimaced. "What was his name—seems like it was—"

"Rosey," I said. "His name was Rosey."

"Yeah." He nodded emphatically and with a grin, said, "That's it. Rosey. He was downing a jug of Thunderbird." He shook his head. "Shame. Harmless old man."

"Yeah." I changed the subject. "Your parole officer says you're doing a good job."

The grin on his face faded into frown of suspicion. "Yeah. I'm doing good."

"What does he think about you delivering laundry to the bars on Sixth Street? Most guys in your shoes are told to stay out of clubs and bars.'

He glanced at Doreen, then with a smug grin, replied, "They just don't want us hanging around there, that's all. As long as it's connected to the job, they got no problem. At least, mine don't."

Doreen frowned. "Isn't Garcia's on Sixth Street?" She winked at me. I grinned, guessing where she was going.

Abdo's smile faded. "Yeah. Why?"

With a nonchalant shrug, she replied, "Oh, nothing.

It's just that we know you were setting up drinks for the house at Garcia's last night. I'd call that hanging around, wouldn't you?"

His face blanched, and a worried frown etched wrinkles in his forehead. He looked around at me, and I nodded. His frown deepened. "Look, so I was down there. One time. Give me a break."

"I don't know." Doreen paused and pulled out her little notebook. As Abdo looked on, she methodically thumbed through the book. "From what we learned, you've been down there more than just last night." She paused, glanced up, then tapped a fingernail on a page in the notebook. "We've even got dates." It was a lie, but he had no way of knowing.

Abdo gulped.

It was my turn to ratchet up the pressure. "You make ten forty-three an hour, four hundred bucks a week, probably closer to three hundred take-home. Yet you drive a Miata. You must be a whiz at money-management, Abdo."

Sweat popped out on his forehead. He gulped hard. He took a step back. "Hey, it's a used one. You can get them cheap."

"How cheap?"

His eyes narrowed. "Look, I don't have to talk to you. You got no—"

"No, you don't," I replied. I pointed to the notebook in Doreen's hand. "We can turn that over to your parole office, and you can explain it all to him."

The balloon of confidence that had inflated his ego suddenly went flat. He seemed to crumple in on himself. "Look. I'm being straight here. I don't know nothing about the fire."

"So, where does all the money come from, Carlos?" Doreen's question was cold and clipped.

He stared at her helplessly for several moments before giving up and dropping his chin to his chest. "All right, but it ain't that much. I been doing some work on the side the last couple weeks for Buck Topper."

Doreen and I looked at each other, each recognizing in the other's face the excitement over the possibility of a break in the case.

I hooked my thumb over my shoulder. "That's where you got the bundle for the Miata?"

"It wasn't no bundle. Five hundred. The dealer's carrying a note on the rest."

Doreen beat me to the punch. "Who's the dealer?"

"Carson's Car Lot on Congress. Jimmy Wills. We go way back so he did me a favor."

I spoke up as she jotted the name in her notebook. "So, what was the job for Buck?"

He hesitated and glanced furtively at Doreen and then back to me. A look of innocence replaced the cunning look on his face. "I don't know everything, but Buck was looking for some kind of glass skull."

I don't know whose jaw dropped open the wider, Doreen's or mine. I clamped my lips shut. "Go on."

"That little wino had stumbled across the skull and

pawned it. Buck hired me to get the ticket from the old man, but I couldn't find him. Next thing I knew, the Hip-Hop burned and Rosey was dead. The pawn ticket wasn't on him, so—"

"Hold on," I said, interrupting. "How did you know the ticket wasn't on him?"

He closed his eyes and shook his head. "This is going to sound suspicious, but I swear, I had nothing to do with torching the Hip-Hop." He paused, then continued. "Like I said, I made my regular deliveries on Monday instead of Tuesday. I kept an eye out for Rosey. I even went back at night looking for him. I saw the fire break out. I started to lose myself, but then I spotted the old man stumble out the back door and fall on the ground. He didn't say nothing when I got to him, so I searched him. He didn't have the pawn ticket."

"So Buck kept you on the payroll to find the ticket or the skull."

"Yeah," he whispered.

I had a nagging feeling that Abdo was holding back on something, but I couldn't put my finger on it. "Were you in the Hip-Hop storeroom in the alley this last Monday?"

"Yeah. The old rummy hung out in there. I figured he might have stashed the ticket somewhere, but I never could find it. Just about the time I finished searching the place, somebody come in, so I got my rear end out of there."

Doreen's face grew hard. "So it was you in there."

Abdo frowned. "Huh?" Suddenly, he realized the implication of her statement. "That was you two?"

I nodded and gently tapped the Band-Aid on my forehead.

He grinned sheepishly. "Hey, man, I'm sorry, but you spooked me big time. I just wanted to get out of there."

"So, you ran into the Red Rabbit, right?"

"Yeah. Buck, he gave me the keys to the back door."

Doreen studied him a moment, then winked at me. "What about the skull? You ever find it?"

He hesitated and glanced at Doreen before he replied. "Naw." He shook his head. "I don't know what the deal is on the skull, but I never could find it. Buck got pretty hot. Made me give him my keys to his back door."

Abdo caught the look Doreen and I exchanged. He frowned. "What?"

"What if I tell you I know you're lying? What if I tell you that we know you found the skull?"

His mouth popped open. "Huh? What are you saying? I told you, I never found the ticket."

Doreen chuckled. "We're not arguing that, Carlos. But we know you found the skull. The only problem, it isn't there any longer."

I thought his eyes were going to pop out of his head. "What?"

"She's right. You found it down at Bernie's Pawnshop."

His swarthy face grew red. He tried to stammer out a response, but he couldn't get past the first word.

I continued. "The skull isn't there. It's gone."

He just stared at us in stunned disbelief.

Doreen eyed him narrowly. "Where were you last night?"

Recovering from his surprise, he shook his head. "Huh? Last night? I was at my place, waiting for Buck to call and tell me what to do next."

"So," Doreen asked, "Buck also knew the skull was at the pawnshop."

What little touch of bravado Abdo possessed quickly fled. "Yeah. He said for me to hang around until he figured out how to get the thing."

She glanced at me and winked.

We watched as Bull Abdo climbed into his Miata, backed it out, and his bandaged forefinger sticking straight up, headed down the street without looking at us as he passed.

"What do you think?" Doreen muttered as we continued to look after him.

"I'm not sure. One thing is certain though, Abdo wasn't at the pawnshop last night."

"Why, because of the dog bites?"

Her perceptiveness impressed me. "Yeah. Last night, Max was all over the guy running from the pawnshop. From the blood in the pawnshop, the dog got some flesh. There were no marks on Abdo's arm."

"Maybe Max got a leg instead of an arm."

I arched an eyebrow. "Could be."

"Or maybe Buck sent someone else besides Abdo."

I looked around at her, impressed. "Maybe. Why don't we talk to him?'

During the drive to the Red Rabbit, Doreen pursed her lips. "How far do we go with Abdo?"

"Hard to say. All we have is an ex-con's word. Let's play it by ear."

"Do you think he torched the place?"

I considered the question. "I don't think so. I don't see what he has to gain. He might not be the brightest light on the tree, but I don't think he's dumb enough to get mixed up with arson and murder. I can see him rousting an old bum, but not murder." I hesitated, then added, "Unless it was by pure accident."

A lecherous grin played over Buck Topper's angular face when he spotted Doreen at my side. "Come on in, you two." He gestured to the almost empty club. "How about a beer?"

"No, thanks," I said, sliding on a stool at the bar. "Have you seen S.S. passing by? I've been looking for him the last couple days. He's dropped out of sight."

Buck's eyes narrowed, then he shrugged. "Naw. S.S. and me don't get along much. You know that. Sure about that beer?"

I closed my eyes and rolled my shoulders. I was almost asleep on my feet. "Just some coffee, and then we need to talk."

He leered at Doreen while he filled my cup and slid it down the bar to me. "What about you, Doreen?"

"Why not? Just a Coke with ice."

Buck arched an eyebrow. "Whatever." He sat a canned Coca-Cola and glass of ice on the counter before her and glanced at me. "Okay, what are we going to talk about?"

I sipped the coffee. "Tell us about Bull Abdo," Doreen said, sliding onto the stool at my side.

The grin faded from his face. "Abdo?" He shrugged. "What about him?"

I was tired and exhausted. With only about thirty minutes sleep, my tail was dragging, and I was in no mood to play games. "Look, Buck. Abdo said you hired him to find a pawn ticket for a glass skull, which meant you knew about the skull two or three days before the fire." I paused, waiting for Buck's response. When he didn't reply, I continued. "He didn't find the ticket, but he did find the skull, and he says he told you about it. Now, is he telling the truth or not? If he is, that means you lied to us."

His smile faded. His gaze darted between us several times. He played for time, time to think. "Lied to you? About what?"

"Monday you said nobody had come into the rear of your club. Abdo says you gave him keys to the back door. It was Abdo who ran over us out in the storeroom. He admitted it. Now, one of you is lying, and when someone lies, they're trying to cover their tails. So who is?"

In a soft, but firm voice, Doreen added in a chilly

tone, "We know much more than you think, Buck. If we're not happy with what we hear, then we'll just turn it all over to the cops and be done with it." She pulled out her little notebook and waved it under his nose. "And what we have here, you don't want the cops to see."

It took all my will power not to laugh at her brass.

His eyes narrowed. He dragged the tip of his tongue over his lips. "All right. Yeah, I lied. I hired Abdo, and he told me where the skull was." He hesitated then continued. "I knew I couldn't get it until the ticket expired, so I had to wait." He paused and drew a deep breath. "Then I heard that Abdo set the fire. Well, I panicked. I didn't want to get mixed up in anything like that."

"Who told you he torched it?"

He grimaced, and in an unconvincing tone replied, "One of my customers. I don't remember who."

"Abdo says he didn't start it."

Buck sneered. "If he didn't, then who did? I just didn't want to get involved with that."

I didn't believe him. Buck had always been able to mix fact and fiction to suit his needs. "That's what I intend to find out. Tell me, Buck. How did you find out about the glass skull?"

The lanky man's shifty eyes studied us. I could see the wheels turning in his head. I decided to jump kick his explanation. "For your information, the skull isn't where Abdo told you."

Anger flashed in his eyes. "What? Why that—"

Doreen chuckled. "Oh, he told you the truth, Buck, but now the skull isn't at the pawnshop any longer."

"That's right," I said. "Now, how did you find out about it?"

His eyes widened in disbelief. "Y-You know where it is?"

Chapter Twenty-two

Doreen smiled at him. "Yes," she replied sweetly. "We know exactly where it is."

A crafty look filled his eyes. "Listen, Tony. If you can get your hands on it, I've got a buyer. A bunch of religious nuts. Coming in to town tomorrow. Claims it was stolen from them, and they'll pay just about anything to get it back. It'll be worth more than you or Doreen can make at that gumshoe job in ten years. We can all retire."

"Is that why you sent someone after it last night?"

"Huh?" He frowned. "Hey, I didn't send nobody anywhere last night." He paused, then with a shrug continued. "Sure, I wanted it. I still do, and—" A crafty look filled his eyes. "I was trying to figure out how to get it, but I didn't do nothing last night." He paused, his

186

face a mask of concentration. "You say someone tried to get it last night?"

"Yeah."

He leaned forward. With a sense of urgency, he whispered, "Jeez! That means someone else knows about it. We have to work fast if we want to make a deal with them guys, Tony."

I studied him suspiciously, wondering if this were just another of his smooth lies. "Why are these people coming to town tomorrow. You don't have the skull?"

He glanced sheepishly at Doreen. He forced a weak laugh. "I told them I could get it."

"Taking a chance, aren't you? What are they going to do if you don't have it?"

He snorted. "What can they do? So, what about it, Tony? Can you guys get it for me? It'll be worth your time."

I glanced at Doreen. Feigning interest, I shrugged. "I don't know, Buck. Maybe. But tell me, how did you find out about the skull?"

Buck drew a deep breath and blew it out slowly. "All right. Now you remember, I ain't made no secret that I wanted to buy the Hip-Hop and Jimmy's Bistro right next door." He gestured to the interior of his club. "Expand this place of mine, you know? Well, one morning a couple weeks ago, I went down to the Hip-Hop before we opened up. I'd seen Getdown go in so I thought I'd get him alone and make another offer. I'd heard on the street that the fat man had turned down one or two offers of a hundred grand, one of them from Abe Romero. I figured on kicking it up to two hundred."

Surprised, I whistled. "Two hundred. That's steep."

"I figured the fat man would go for it."

I studied him carefully. "Can you swing that kind of bundle?"

A shrewd gleam filled his eyes and a faint smile touched his thin lips. "It would have been hard, but I could have swung it."

He glanced at Doreen and continued. "The front was empty. I figured Getdown was in his office, so I headed back there. The door was open. I could hear talking." He paused, and in all fairness to Buck, I'll admit a sheepish grin did play over his face as he continued. "So, I listened." He shrugged when he spotted the knowing grin on my face. "Hey, it don't hurt to listen. After all, you never know what you can pick up."

Doreen chuckled. "So, what did you hear?"

"Whoever he was, this dude had a crystal skull he wanted to sell to Getdown for ten Gs. He claimed the right collectors would fork over three million or more for it. Getdown figured it was a scam. He nixed the offer." He shrugged. "If I'd knowed then what I know now, I would of collared that dude myself."

I interrupted. "If it was worth that much, why did the guy want to sell it for only ten grand?"

Buck grunted. "I ain't got no proof, but I got the feeling the dude was on the lam. He said something about the next bus out of town. Anyway, when I heard the dude start to leave, I ducked into the storeroom. After the guy left, Getdown sent Ivory to follow him and get the skull."

"Ivory?" I frowned.

Buck explained. "One of Getdown's boys, Ivory Washington." He tapped his finger to his temple. "Slow as molasses up here. I think his first name is Leander. You saw him the other day when you talked to Getdown. Small guy, bald head."

I nodded, remembering the light-complexioned young man.

Buck continued. "Look, I know the fat man. He'll chisel any way he can for a buck. My guess is that he sent Ivory to find where the dude holed up and rip off the skull."

His little theory tallied with Goofyfoot's story about Rosey finding the skull in a Dumpster behind the Blackhawk Towers. The dude could have hidden it there, planning on returning to retrieve it. So, why hadn't he?

We were beginning to pick up more and more loose ends.

"This guy. You get a look at him?"

With an indifferent shrug, Buck grunted. "Kinda. Small. Had a big nose. I ain't got no prejudices, but he looked like one of those Jew-boys. That's about it."

Doreen spoke up. "You said you had a buyer."

His eyes narrowed. "Yeah. I can get us a good price."

Casually, I asked, "How did you find a buyer?"

He grinned slyly. "I got contacts."

I thought about the names J. C. Towers had given us, Carl Simmons of Dallas, George Bernard of Denver, and Rosalind Attenborough in London. I had no doubt just a little deeper digging online would turn up their names as well as the names of other collectors. "Who?"

A fair sneer curled one side of his lips as he looked at Doreen, then back at me. "Don't worry, I got them." He paused. "Well?"

His question jerked me back to the present. "Well, what?"

"Do we have a deal? I mean, can you get me the skull?"

I downed the last of the coffee and tossed a sawbuck on the counter. "Sorry. No can do."

I slid into the passenger seat in Doreen's Jag and leaned my head back and closed my eyes.

While Doreen buckled up, she remarked, "You must be exhausted."

"Yeah," I muttered. And that was the last I remember until we pulled into the parking lot at the office.

She parked by my Silverado. "Can you make it home?"

The few minutes sleep had done wonders, at least wonders enough that I figured I could handle the twenty minutes to my apartment on Peyton-Gin Road. "Yeah. Thanks. See you in the morning. After a good night's sleep, we'll sit down and figure just where we stand."

On the way home, I suddenly remembered the date with Janice later that evening. I hadn't heard from her since I had come face to face with her at the signal light on Congress Street the night before. I had planned to show up at her place at 8:00, figuring if she were still angry from the night before, she'd let me know then.

"At least," I muttered as I pulled into the driveway, "I can get a little sleep first."

Locking my apartment door behind me, I stumbled to the kitchen. The chicken salad and tea for lunch at the deli was down to my toes. I was too tired to be hungry. I eyed the half-full bottle of bourbon, then drew a glass of water and chugged it down.

The phone rang. It was Janice. When I heard her voice, my life passed before my eyes. I steeled myself for her tirade.

Before I could stammer or stutter, she apologized for last night. "I realized later that you and your partner were probably on the way to your surveillance. Anyway, as much as I hate to, I have to postpone tonight. Aunt Beatrice wants me to fly to Dallas with her for a few days. I'll call when I get back. You understand, don't you, Tony? You aren't upset, are you?"

Magnanimous me, I replied, "No. Oh no. I was really looking forward to it, but I understand. Those things happen. Have fun. I'll manage."

After we hung up, I breathed a sigh of relief. I nuked some milk for A.B., dished out some nuggets for him, and then shuffled to my bedroom where I undressed, passed on a shower, and slid under the covers.

And died.

*   *   *

Next thing I knew, it was 5:30. I lay staring at the ceiling, my body still tired, but my brain working.

We had a plethora of loose ends, but nothing to connect them.

Truth was, we weren't much closer to finding the torch man than we had been on Monday, three days earlier.

I knew where the crystal skull came in. It was worth a bundle, and while I had no proof, there was no question in my mind that whoever torched the Hip-Hop also killed Rosey, perhaps in an effort to find the skull.

Suddenly, the phone rang, breaking the pristine silence of the morning and interrupting my poorly disguised efforts at playing Sherlock Holmes. It was Doreen. "Tony, you watching local news?"

"No, why?"

"Turn it on. Channel eight."

I flipped it on and froze.

Police cruisers were parked at every angle around Towers' Jewelers, and an animated reporter announced that during the night, a single burglar had held an employee at gunpoint and taken several hundred thousand dollars of merchandise.

The news hit me between the eyes. I knew exactly what was missing, and immediately I started calling

J. C. Towers every vile name I could think of and then some.

The diminutive man wanted the skull. That fact was obvious, but would he go to such an extent to possess it? I found that hard to believe, but still, after several years dealing with the human race, I had witnessed more than one person throw his life away because he couldn't control his greed.

And to toss another log on the firestorm, Mrs. Bernie called, demanding in her inimitable crude manner to know just what had happened to her expletive, expletive, expletive skull. And it certainly did nothing to salve her temper when I told her I had no idea what had taken place.

Naturally, Doreen and I couldn't get anywhere near J. C. Towers until the police completed their initial investigation, so we sat in the parking lot in my pickup, sipping coffee and waiting until the cops left.

After informing me she had contacted Jimmy Willis at Carson's Car Lot, and he verified Bull Abdo's version of the Miata purchase, she continued. "Last night, I couldn't sleep," she said, staring out the window. "So I pulled out my notes. I ran across a couple things that puzzled me. Maybe you can make some sense of them."

I scooted around in the seat. "Such as?"

She flipped open her small notebook. "Okay. When we talked to Abdo yesterday, he said he made his biweekly delivery to the clubs on Sixth Street on Tuesdays and Fridays." I nodded and she continued. "Abdo said on Monday, he picked up all the dirty laundry and dropped off towels, tablecloths, and the fancy uniforms the waitstaff of the Hip-Hop were to wear."

A tiny glimmer of understanding flickered in the back of my head. One of the worst mistakes a PI can make is not to take time to reflect and analyze gathered information. Our investigation had been so intense the last three days, I'd failed to take that time. "Go on."

"When we talked to Sillery, he said among his property lost in the fire on Tuesday were towels, tablecloths, and some fancy uniforms he had bought for his people to start wearing."

I was puzzled. "And?"

"And," she replied, her black eyes glittering with excitement, "he also claimed that on that Monday and Tuesday, he was in Dallas at the Somalia Sunrise Club auditioning rap groups for the Hip-Hop."

I nodded, still uncertain as to her point.

She continued. "So, regular pickup and delivery for laundry is Tuesday and Fridays on Sixth Street. That week, Abdo delivered early, on Monday. If Getdown was in Dallas, how did he know a new delivery of laundry was in the back? With the new uniforms."

Suddenly, I understood exactly what she was trying to say. "Yeah. The ones he bought from the laundry for his people to—"

"Wear. So, how did he know the uniforms were delivered a week early if he was in Dallas?"

Chapter Twenty-three

At that moment, two officers emerged from the jewelry store and climbed into their cruiser.

We waited, but the black and white didn't move. "Come on," I muttered impatiently. "Take off."

Her eyes fixed on the black-and-white cruiser, Doreen muttered, "Do you think he was at the Somalia Sunrise?"

"Huh?" I looked around. "What?"

"Getdown Joe. Do you think he was really at the Somalia Sunrise Club in Dallas?"

I had to admit, she was bright and perceptive. "Makes you wonder, doesn't it? Maybe we ought to give the club a call."

A satisfied grin played over her lips. "I'll do it."

"And while you're taking care of that, there's another thing we need to find out. Remember last night when

Buck told us about the guy offering the skull to Get-down?"

"Yes."

"What happened to that guy? Where'd he go?"

She nodded. "I wondered that myself. If the skull was so valuable, he wouldn't run off and leave it."

"Not if he had a choice."

She studied me a moment. "You think . . ." Her voice trailed off and her forehead wrinkled with concern.

At that moment, the police cruiser sped away. I opened my door. "Let's go. We'll tie this up later."

Crime scene tapes were still strung around the vault when we entered.

J. C. Towers gaped at us when we barged into his of-fice followed by a stuttering secretary who had tried to stop us. "Boudreaux," he muttered.

My eyes narrowed. "All right, Towers. What hap-pened?"

He waved his secretary from the room. "I'll call if I need you, Miss Heath. Close the door, please." He ges-tured to the leather chairs in front of his ponderous desk and then plopped down in his. He fished a hand-kerchief from his pocket and wiped at the perspiration beading on his forehead. Nervously, his gaze darted back and forth between Doreen and me. His Adam's apple bobbed. "I know what you're thinking."

I snorted. "If you did, you wouldn't be sitting there

facing me. In fact, I wouldn't be surprised if Mrs. Bernie kicked that door open and came after you with Max!"

His thin face blanched, and he swallowed hard. He punched the speaker on his desk phone. "Miss Heath, send Mister Sheffield in. Immediately!" He looked up at us when he clicked off. "Sheffield can tell you what happened. He was the one who was forced to open the safe."

Moments later, the door opened, and a pale-faced man about my height opened the door. If it were possible, he was even thinner than Towers, and if Towers turned sideways, he wouldn't even throw a shadow. "You wanted me, Mister Towers?"

"Come in, George." He introduced us, then said, "Tell them what took place last night." Sheffield frowned, but Towers nodded. "It's all right."

"If you say so, sir." He addressed us. "This morning just after four, I awakened to find a man wearing a ski mask holding a gun on me."

A ski mask! I remembered the driver of the Lincoln who had tried to smash me between two Dumpsters behind the Blackhawk Towers. Could it have been the same person? Of course, I knew that was a stretch for just about everyone on Sixth Street had his own wardrobe of ski masks.

Sheffield continued. "Well, not exactly like a ski mask. It was like one, but it didn't have a top. He had an Afro haircut. He forced me to dress and said he'd kill me if I didn't get the keys to the store."

An Afro? That narrows it to fifty or sixty thousand, I told myself wryly. "Why you?"

Sheffield shrugged. "I suppose he knew that I opened and closed the safe."

Towers confirmed Sheffield's remark. "Only the two of us know the combination, and I'd trust George with everything I have."

Doreen chuckled. "Looks like you already have."

I gestured to Sheffield. "Then what?"

"Then he blindfolded me, and put me in his car."

Remembering the yellow Jeep with black fenders and lightning bolts, I questioned him. "What kind of car?"

He shrugged. "I don't know. I told you, I was blind-folded."

"Maybe so," Doreen interjected, "but, did you have to step up into it or down; was it rough riding or easy riding; noisy or quiet?"

Sheffield pondered the question. "It was a big car, comfortable. Is that what you mean?"

"Yeah," I replied, knowing he wasn't talking about the yellow-and-black Jeep. On the other hand, the lifter could have stolen the larger vehicle just in case some-one spotted him. "Anything else?"

His brow knit in concentration. "I had to step down into it, and it had automatic locks because I could hear them click." He paused and then shrugged. "That's all I can remember about the car, except it had that new smell, you know what I mean?"

"That's fine, Mister Sheffield," said Doreen. "So what happened then?"

"When we reached the store, he took off my blindfold. He made me turn off the alarms and then open the safe. Then he blindfolded me again and tied me up."

"Before he blindfolded you again though, you saw him."

"Yes." He shot a glance at Towers, then continued. "But he was still wearing the ski mask."

"But, he had an Afro."

Towers cleared his throat. "Tell them exactly what you told the police, George. They're here to help us."

I had a feeling Towers' last remark was just a tad gratuitous. I wondered why at the time.

Sheffield glanced uncomfortably at the carpeted floor. "Yes." He hesitated. "I think the hair looked like it, but the other features—you know, his lips and nose—they didn't look African." He paused and shrugged. "Anyway, after he blindfolded me, I heard him going through the vault, and then he left." He nodded to J. C. Towers. "I managed to free myself and immediately called Mister Towers."

The diminutive jeweler added, "I rushed right down here, inspected the vault, and we called the police."

I studied them a moment. I looked at Towers, my eyes asking the question foremost in my mind.

He dropped his eyes and nodded. "Yes."

"Was the skull the only thing missing?"

Sheffield shot Towers a furtive glance as the diminutive storeowner replied, "No. We checked our inventory. There's almost two million in uncut diamonds missing."

I whistled softly. "How much would they be worth on the street?"

Towers arched an eyebrow. "Full value. It would be next to impossible to identify them. If they were some of the macle-twin crystals, it would be simple. But they were primarily the spherical crystals from Brazil."

Taking a step toward Towers, I said, "I want to see the vault."

He hesitated.

"The police have finished. And I want to look at it."

Ducking under the tapes, I entered the vault. The stainless steel shelf on which the skull had rested was empty. Along one side of the vault was a bank of drawers. "What are those?"

Towers explained. "That's where we place our inventory of stones every night."

I noticed that only two drawers were open, one in the top row and the other in the bottom row.

Towers' licked his lips and stared up at me nervously. "Is there anything else?"

I studied the interior of the vault a moment longer. Something was out of place, but I had no idea what. After a few years dealing with the underbelly of society, lawmen and PIs develop a sixth sense of sorts that sets off an alarm. And that alarm was clanging in my head. I had the sneaking suspicion that J. C. Towers and George Sheffield were holding something back.

Back in the pickup I put in a call to Billy Joe Martin at the Travis County Morgue. While waiting, I had Doreen use her cell phone to call information in Dallas for the Somalia Sunrise Club. "Find out if they were auditioning rap groups Monday and Tuesday of last week."

She grinned and nodded. "You bet."

My connection came along. "Martin. County Morgue."

"Hey, Billy Joe. It's Tony. I got a question."

"You're turning into a good customer, Tony. What is this, the second time this week?"

"Gotta make sure you guys are earning your money." I paused. "Listen, you got any stiffs from a couple weeks back that you haven't put a name on? White guy."

He thought a moment. "Nope. The last one was the wino you stuck a label on."

"I'm trying to locate a short man with a big nose. Probably Jewish."

"Yeah. I remember him. We got him Monday or Tuesday. Hermie Abraham, out of New York. Fell off the balcony on his room on the tenth floor of the Blackhawk Towers."

I whistled softly. No wonder the manager at the Blackhawk was nervous when I approached him. I drew a deep breath. I couldn't blame him. It would never do for the public to know one of his guests jumped from a balcony.

Still, I told myself, *we've got us a ski mask, Blackhawk Towers, Dumpsters.* Maybe some of my loose ends were starting to come together. I thanked Billy Joe and punched off just as Doreen clicked her cell close and shook her head slowly.

"No auditions, and the club just reopened this week after being closed for a month by the ATF."

We stared at each other several seconds.

She arched an eyebrow. "Now where do we go?"

I considered our next step. Speaking with Getdown might be a little premature even though we knew he lied about being in Dallas or at least about the auditions. And Doreen was also right when she surmised that he had to be in the back room of the Hip-Hop sometime after Monday when Abdo had delivered the laundry that included the uniforms that were not due until the following week. Otherwise, how could he have known the uniforms were there?

Perhaps, Ivory Washington could be our next step. I was curious as to what he knew about Hermie Abraham's demise. Of course, finding him might be tricky. Maybe that could wait until tomorrow.

"Let's head back to the office. I want to check my e-mail. Besides, it'll give us time to collect our thoughts."

She shrugged. "Fine with me."

At the office, I checked my personal e-mail. Mostly spam: health enhancements, singles opportunities, even a couple notes from some third world countries generously offering me a share of forty million dollars and all they needed was my social security number and bank account.

Then my eyes lit up when I spotted a message from J. Adkins-Manor. "Here it is," I muttered, waving Doreen to my desk. "Take a look."

Mister Boudreaux.

In response to your inquiry regarding the Nelson-Vines Crystal Skull, there was a second skull of such quality and technique that is cut against the natural axis of the crystal.

The skull was the religious centerpiece of the Mesoamerican Lemurian sect, but it disappeared twenty-eight years ago.

If this is the Lemurian Crystal Skull, I would recommend efforts be made to return it to the sect.

Being a close acquaintance of the Vines, I mentioned your e-mail to them. Despite my efforts to discourage them with respect to the Mesoamerican Lemurian sect, the Vines would be willing to make a most generous offer for the skull.

Doreen was leaning over me, reading the message. She had one hand on my shoulder and the other on the desk, and the fragrance of her perfume enveloped me. What was so remarkable was that this was the first time I whiffed the aroma of perfume on her.

She pointed at the monitor. "What's that Mesoamerican Lemurian religious stuff?"

I shrugged. "I've heard some about it. A bunch of fanatics. Like those suicide crazies in the Middle East. Crazy, and scary. Let's see what we can find."

An online search turned up several articles concerning the Mesoamerican Lemurians, a religious culture that existed in the Pacific Ocean. According to one article:

Once a tropical village society involving a land mass from Hawaii to Los Angeles before sinking beneath the Pacific Ocean, its society was made up of pods of clairvoyant seers, oracles, and holy people to whom the members of the group could turn for guidance and justice, the latter being dispensed by squads of Holy Warriors.

The International Headquarters for the Mesoamerican Lemurians is located in Los Angeles. The vibration of that ancient land, which was creatively based, is ample explanation as to why there has been such an influx of higher consciousness ideas from the West Coast.

I raised a skeptical eyebrow. Higher consciousness, my hind leg.

Doreen whistled softly and stood up. "I don't believe any of that nonsense."

Looking up at her, I replied, "Remember what Buck said. He had some religious nuts that wanted the skull. Maybe this is them." I shook my head, remembering some of the chilling stories I'd heard about the group over the years. "And maybe for his own sake, it won't be them."

She studied the monitor a few moments, then blew out through her lips slowly. "Then maybe we've stumbled onto something big."

"Can't tell," I replied. "Can't tell."

She cleared her throat. "I think we should head back to Sixth Street. This joker, Ivory, the one that Buck heard Getdown Joe send after that Abraham guy who offered to sell him the skull—he's the one we need to talk to." She rubbed the back of her neck. "I just got a feeling he's the key to all this."

Why not? So much for tomorrow. I rose from my chair. "Let's get with it."

Outside in the parking lot, Janice Coffman-Morrison was sitting in her blue Miata with the top down, engine running. She gave Doreen a look that could only be described as scorching, then smiled sweetly at me. "Hello, Tony," she said in a soft and gentle voice liberally dosed with strychnine.

Chapter Twenty-four

I've always been fairly glib, which is the politically correct way of saying I can lie with the best of them, a definite plus for a PI, but at that instant, the proverbial cat had my tongue. I stammered and stuttered.

Her smile grew wider. "Aunt Beatrice canceled the trip. I tried to call you, but you weren't answering." She paused and smiled sweetly at Doreen. "Where's your manners, Tony? Aren't you going to introduce me to your partner?" The skepticism she placed on the word partner was obvious.

Finally, I managed a reply, not too eloquent, but in my flustered state, it was all I could manage. "Janice!"

Doreen saved my life. Later I figured she responded as she did because of her own turbulent history in previous relationships. Whatever the reason, she smiled brightly, stepped forward, and with an amiable bubble in her voice, extended her hand to Janice. "Hi. I'm Doreen Patterson, and you've got to be Janice, Tony's good friend. He's told me so much about you, I'd know you anywhere. I've been looking forward to meeting you, but Tony has kept us hopping the last few days."

Whatever Janice had expected, that wasn't it. Taken aback by Doreen's affable and flattering words, Janice automatically took her hand. She glanced up at me, her brows momentarily knit in confusion.

One of the traits I've always admired about Janice, however, was her ability not to convey her feelings in a confused situation. More than once, I had seen her confront circumstances that would have caused the average woman to pull out her hair, but Janice, after a moment or so to collect her composure, simply faced it with the casual aplomb of the very rich.

I suppose in the finishing school she attended in Atlanta there was probably had a course titled "Cool Composure in Any Situation." And if there were, and if she took the course, Janice got an A+ in it.

A warm smile leaped to her lips, and she replied, "Tony told me he had a new partner, and I have so been wanting to meet you." Her dark eyes flicked at me before she continued. "Perhaps you can come out to the ranch with Tony one day."

Doreen gushed. "I'd love to, but when I'm not working on the job, I spend my time researching a historical anthology I've been writing for the last five years. Besides, I'd just be a third wheel with you two."

"Oh, no. There is so much to do. Why—"

If anyone felt like a third wheel, I did, standing there listening to the two of them lying so sweetly to each other, and each knowing exactly what the other was doing. Such parrying and repartee was the stuff of great pirate movies. It never made sense to me, but then, I'm just a thick-headed male.

Finally, Janice addressed me. "Aunt Beatrice is planning a reception Sunday at the ranch, Tony. She wanted me to ask you if you could create one of those delicious Louisiana dishes for the table. People raved over your court bouillon last time."

I nodded hastily, unsure just what had prompted her to be so amiable, but I certainly didn't want to waste time figuring it out. "You bet. What time?"

"Two, but you probably need to be there by noon."

"No problem."

Her eyes twinkled. "And can you bring the little car?"

"Yeah. Sunday, noon." From the corner of my eye, I saw Doreen look at me.

Her smile grew wider, and then she did something completely out of character for her. She reached out her carefully manicured hand to me. I took it. Pursing her lips, she drew me down to her.

Ears burning, I touched my lips to hers lightly, surprised and not just a little confused over the kiss. Janice had never been so demonstrative in public.

We watched as Janice drove away.

Doreen chuckled. "Well, she made that pretty clear, didn't she?"

"You mean about Sunday? Yeah, she did."

She eyed me a moment, a look of amusement on her face. Finally, she shook her head. "You men can be so thick-headed at times. No wonder we leave you."

I frowned. "What are you talking about?"

"Never mind." She shook her head, still smiling.

"Well, thanks anyway," I said.

"For what?"

"For getting me out of a sticky situation. She was really burned up with me."

"Why?"

I frowned. "I'm not sure. But thanks anyway."

Doreen chuckled. "Forget it. Been there, done that. Besides, we're partners."

I glanced at her. She was still looking after Janice. I grinned. "Yeah. Partners."

"Sweet girl," Doreen said.

I frowned at her, surprised by the sincerity in her voice. I'm not sure what I expected, but sincerity wasn't it.

With a shrug, I replied, "Yeah. She is a nice person. A little different, but we get along."

Still looking after Janice, Doreen observed, "Rich, huh?"

I chuckled. "Richer than the Queen of England."

She looked around at me quizzically. "How did you two hook up?"

Laughing, I pointed to my pickup. "I'll tell you about it on the way."

As I buckled my seat belt, I began my story. "Janice's aunt is Beatrice Morrison, owner and CEO of Chalk Hills Distillery west of Austin. Janice is her only family."

Doreen arched an eyebrow. "Makes it nice for you, huh?"

With a wry grin, I shook my head. "That, partner, would never work. Been married once, no kids. Don't figure on trying it again." During the remainder of the drive down to Sixth Street, I filled Doreen in on the turbulent relationship Janice and I enjoyed, and sometimes endured.

"So, what's this dish you're supposed to whip up for her aunt's reception?"

Laughing, I explained. "You know how these rich people are. They like exotic dishes, and to them, the everyday meals I grew up with back in Louisiana are exotic. Don't ask me why, they just are. Last time, I whipped up a pot of catfish court bouillon. Between you and me," I said with a wink, "I think it was the fancy word, court bouillon, that got the rich dudes."

"Is that what you're going to fix this time?"

"Maybe." I flexed my fingers about the wheel. "Or maybe some frogleg jambalaya."

Doreen exclaimed. "Frogleg jambalaya! That sounds—oh, yucky."

I grinned. "Don't knock it until you try it. In fact,

give me your address, and after I whip up a batch Sunday morning, I'll drop you off a plate."

She shook her head. "No, thanks."

"How about some *jambe de grenouille* jambalaya?"

A frown wrinkled her forehead. "What's that?"

I laughed. "Same thing. It's French. Rest assured, if I take frogleg jambalaya, I'll make sure to call it *jambe de grenouille* jambalaya."

She shivered. "Thanks anyway."

"Well then," I replied, eyeing her with amusement. "How about, say, chicken jambalaya?"

"That sounds better." She nodded. "But don't make a special trip. Just bring me a plate to the office Monday."

"No problem. That was fast thinking."

She frowned at me. "What?"

I grinned. "The research business."

"It's the truth."

"Huh?" I shot her a puzzled glance.

"For the last several years, I've been putting together an anthology of biographies for the signers of the Declaration of Independence. That is what I do on my time off."

I whistled and shook my head. "I'm impressed."

She smiled warmly. "Thank you. Now, answer me this. What's the little car Janice was talking about?"

"Little car? Oh." I laughed. "Last year in Vicksburg, I bought a Model T Ford. I keep it in my garage and take it out on sunny days. Janice loves to ride in it."

A flash of color caught my eyes, and I hit the brakes

and turned sharply into a parking lot just before we reached Sixth Street.

"What the—" Doreen exclaimed, grabbing the crash grip on the dashboard.

Sitting on the edge of the parking lot was a yellow Jeep with black fenders and lightning bolts on the side. "Over there. That Jeep. It was behind us yesterday when we hauled Towers and the skull to his store. It was driving past the store when we left."

I pulled up behind the Jeep and climbed out. I laid my hand on the hood. It was still warm. Pulling out my cell phone, I punched in the office number. Al Grogan, our resident Sherlock Holmes, answered.

As I climbed in the pickup, I explained, "Al, I need an ID on a license, fast. Can you get it for me?"

"I'm booting up now."

I gave him the number and waited. Doreen held up her fingers, crossed.

Moments later, Al came back. "Austin number. Belongs to Leander Z. Washington, 1144 Festival Beach."

I repeated the address as Doreen wrote it down. "Thanks, Al." I punched off. "That guy who works for Getdown, Ivory. Didn't Buck say his name was Leander?"

Doreen nodded. "Yes."

I snapped my fingers. "Bingo! The Jeep belongs to Ivory Washington. After we see Getdown, let's run this guy down." I glanced inside the Jeep. The keys were still in the ignition. I grabbed them.

The last parking slot on Sixth Street was in front of Neon Larry's. I stuck my head in Larry's. He nodded when he spotted me. "Hey, Tony. Come on in for a beer."

I declined. "Maybe later. You seen Getdown or S.S.?"

He nodded. "Yeah. S.S. was in here a few minutes ago. Said he'd be right back after he took care of some business." He laughed. "He sure is getting popular."

His reply took me by surprise. S.S. was as much a night person as I was a morning one. This time of day was breakfast time for him, lunchtime for the rest of us. I glanced at my watch and lifted an eyebrow. "Kinda early for him, huh?"

Larry laughed and smoothed at his gray ponytail. "Yep. He usually don't come in until about eight. He's been off the last couple days I figure he decided to come in early to make up for the time he took off."

In all the years I had known him, S.S. had seldom taken time off unless he was ill. "He been sick?"

A patron entered and climbed on a stool by the bar. "Nope," said Larry, moving away from us. "Looked fine."

"Did he say where he was going?"

"Check with Buck. Last Monday, S.S. said he was going down to the Red Rabbit to see Buck about some investment they had going. He might have gone down there. If you run across him, tell him that the guy what delivers our laundry is looking for him too. He left just before you two come in."

With a frown, I nodded and glanced at Doreen. She

was just as puzzled as I. What did Bull Abdo have to do with S.S. Thibeaux? And what investment was so enticing that S.S. would put aside his long-standing hatred for Buck?

The Red Rabbit was only eight or ten doors down the street from Neon Larry's, but the journey took us several minutes, for we paused along the way, tossing shaky ideas around, hoping to come up with some logical answers.

Doreen frowned at me. "What kind of investment do you think S.S. had with Buck Topper?"

I shrugged. "I've got no idea any more than I can figure out what Abdo wants with S.S."

Doreen paused and stared unseeing into space. "All right. We know Abdo worked for Buck."

"Yeah. To run down the crystal skull, which he did."

"About the same time S.S. didn't show up for work for the last couple days, the skull disappeared." She stared coolly into my eyes, her own hinting at the same questions tumbling through my head.

"Convenient, huh?"

She shrugged. "Very. Could Abdo be looking for S.S. over the skull? Could it be S.S. is mixed up in all this too?"

I didn't want to think that, but then I had no explanation why Abdo was looking for S.S. nor an answer as to why he was doing business with someone he hated. "I don't know," I said. "Let's take it a step further. We know Abdo found the skull. We know he told Buck about it."

Doreen nodded emphatically. "Think about it. Abdo stayed home waiting for Buck to call. He didn't. Maybe he sent someone else out to the pawnshop. If S.S. is mixed up in this, maybe he's the one Buck sent."

I liked S.S., but as much as I didn't want to admit it, her theory made sense to me.

"So what do you think?" she looked at me hopefully.

Arching an eyebrow, I said, "I think we've built us a really nice little theory here. The only problem is that we don't have any hard evidence to support even a single little premise of our speculation."

There were half-a-dozen or so patrons inside the Red Rabbit.

"I should have known," I muttered, spotting Getdown at the back of the room gobbling down cheeseburgers.

With his shiny black hair hanging down on his forehead, Buck sat at the table with him, and the two seemed engrossed in their conversation, which stopped abruptly as we approached.

Getdown licked the grease off his sausage-like fingers and grinned up at us. "Well, you find out who torched the place?"

I pulled out a chair for Doreen and one for myself. "Getting closer," I replied, glancing at Buck who was eyeing me warily. "That's one of the reasons I'm here. There's a few things we need to straighten out before we go any further."

Getdown frowned and shot a puzzled look at Buck who brushed his greasy hair from his eyes and scooted back from the table. "You guys talk. You need anything, just give me a yell."

"Before you leave, Buck. You seen S.S. around?"

He shook his head. "S.S.? That jerk? What would I see him for?"

Doreen shot me a furtive look. I raised an eyebrow, and she nodded almost imperceptibly.

"Never mind. Thanks anyway."

"No problem. Like I said, shout if you need anything."

After Buck was out of earshot, Getdown frowned. "Now what's this all about?"

Resting my elbows on the table, I leaned forward and narrowed my eyes. "Look, when we take on a client, we do the best we can with the information we have. But when one of our clients deliberately lies to us, then I'm ready to take that lie and stick it where it hurts most."

A cagey gleam filled his small, pig eyes. "What are you talking about, Boudreaux?"

"You lied to us, Getdown. You weren't in Dallas when your club burned down. You were here in Austin."

Chapter Twenty-five

He protested. "I don't know what kind of pills you've been popping, but whatever they is has gots you seeing things. I told you I was up in Dallas at the Somalia Sunrise Club."

I leaned back and folded my arms across my chest. "That's a fine trick. Tell me, Getdown, how do you audition rap groups when there aren't any rap groups around?"

A flicker of surprise glittered in his eyes momentarily, then faded. "Whoever told you that was flying higher than a kite."

"Maybe so, but it was the same one who told us that the Somalia Sunrise had been closed down for a month. Just reopened a couple days ago." I leaned forward and fixed my eyes on his. "Besides, how did you know the

217

uniforms you ordered from the laundry burned if you
didn't see them on Monday?"

He frowned, but his small eyes shifted nervously
from Doreen to me. "What's that you're saying? What
uniforms? I don't know what you're talking about."

"Yes, you do," Doreen said, pulling out that ubiquitous notebook of hers like a shotgun and thumbing
through the pages. "When we first interviewed you, you
said—" she paused, then read from her notebook. "You
said, 'I had a backroom full of beer and wine plus all of
my cloth goods.' When Tony questioned you as to cloth
goods, you said, 'towels for the bar and restrooms,
tablecloths, and the new uniforms for my people.' " She
snapped the notebook shut. "Those are the uniforms
we're talking about."

I took over. "They were delivered on Monday before
the fire on Tuesday. The only ones who could have
known about the uniforms were those who had been in
the storeroom."

Sweat beaded on his fat forehead and floppy cheeks
and rolled down the folds of sagging flesh about his
neck, staining the collar of his pale-yellow silk shirt.

I nodded to Doreen's notebook. "Cops might be interested in that little book of yours, what do you think?"

She chuckled. "It might open their eyes."

Getdown Joe dragged the tip of his tongue across
his lips. "All right. So I was in town that Monday. After
the bar closed down that night, I come in to pick up
some scratch for a trip I was taking the next day. I saw

the receipts for the laundry delivery on the desk. That's how I knew the uniforms was there."

A tenuous thought hit me, then vanished. I glanced at Doreen.

She frowned. "What?"

Joe hesitated, puzzled.

I shook my head and made him repeat himself, hoping I could latch on to that wraithlike thought.

"What?"

"What you just said about coming in to pick up some cash."

He frowned at Doreen, then shrugged. "Like I said, I was in town, but I didn't torch the place. After the boys closed up for the night, I come in and picked up some cash for a trip to Denver the next day. The receipt for the laundry delivery was on the desk. That's how I knew the uniforms was back there."

There was the wispy thought again, and again still evading substance. "Go on. Then what?"

"I caught the six o'clock flight out to Denver Tuesday morning. I got back Wednesday morning. So, when the fire started, I was out of town." He must have seen the skepticism on my face, for he added, "And I can prove it."

I rolled my eyes. "Sure you can."

He nodded emphatically. "I was in Denver, at a meeting with a guy."

For a moment, I studied him. Sighing deeply, I shook my head. "Okay, what guy?"

He pressed his lips together doggedly.

I held out my hands on either side in frustration. "Me or the cops, Joe. Me or the cops."

He nodded. "Okay, okay. A dude named Bernard, George Bernard." He hesitated. "We—ah—we had business to discuss."

Doreen and I looked at each other in surprise. According to J. C. Towers, George Bernard was one of the three most notable collectors of crystal skulls in the world. If Getdown was with Bernard on Tuesday, he couldn't have torched his club.

Trying to keep the excitement from my voice, I asked, "What business did you have with Bernard?"

Getdown grew tight-lipped. "Just business."

My next words hit him between the eyes. "About the crystal skull?" He gaped at us, and I continued. "We know about the skull, Joe. What I want to know is your connection with it."

He stammered a moment, and before he could reply, I continued. "I've got enough on you that the police would be more than interested in taking a look."

His eyes narrowed. "You ain't got nothing. You can't prove nothing."

"No? I know a guy named Abraham tried to sell you the skull, and you sent your boy, Ivory, to follow him. That night, Abraham fell, or maybe he was pushed from his tenth floor balcony. Too bad, because you still couldn't get your hands on the skull. Then somehow, you must have found the skull at Bernie's Pawnshop. Of course, without the ticket, you couldn't get to it."

"Then yesterday, when we transported the skull to the jewelers, your boy, Ivory, followed us. And surprise, surprise, the jewelry store was broken into last night and the skull along with a couple million in uncut diamonds was taken."

Getdown Joe's eyes grew wide. The white around his black pupils contrasted sharply with his dark skin. "What makes you think that?" He demanded. "How do you know it was Ivory?"

"His Jeep. His yellow-and-black Jeep. The same one parked at the lot two blocks north of here."

Getdown sputtered. "The Jeep was stolen. If you don't believe me, call the cops. Ivory done reported it Monday."

I winked at Doreen whose lips were twisted into a skeptical grin. "You bet. Next you'll be telling us the cow really did jump over the moon."

He frowned. "Huh?"

"Forget it."

At that moment, a short, lanky black man with a bald head and wearing a loose-fitting tank top and baggy shorts that sagged within six or eight inches of his bare ankles entered the Red Rabbit. I recognized Ivory.

Doreen nodded to his unblemished arms. Whatever else Ivory might have done, there were no wounds to suggest he was the one who broke into the pawnshop a couple nights back.

Getdown waved him over and gestured to us. "Ivory.

You get your tail over here and tell this dude about your car. He don't believe it was stolen."

The light-complexion man frowned. "What's that you say, Mister Joe?"

Getdown pointed to me. "This PI don't believe your car was stolen."

Ivory looked up at me blankly and in a dull monotone devoid of any expression, said, "Yes, sir, mister. That Jeep of mine was done stole last Monday. When I told Mister Joe about it, he told me to report it to the law." He shrugged. "I did, but me, I don't figure I'll ever see it again."

Getdown grunted. "Don't be too sure, Ivory. These two here say they saw it at the Munkres' parking lot a couple blocks north of here."

A puzzled frown wrinkled Ivory's forehead. He stared at Getdown, not comprehending the fat man's words. "What's that, Mister Joe? Are you kidding me?"

Getdown shook his head and with a soft grin, replied, "No. Your Jeep is at Munkres' parking lot."

The lean man's eyes lit up as he finally understood Getdown's words. I glanced at Doreen who arched an eyebrow. I nodded. Buck Topper wasn't far off base. Ivory was slow.

"I reckon I ought to go up and be certain, don't you think so, Mister Joe?"

"Sure, Ivory. Get up there. If it's your Jeep, then call the police and tell them you found it. You hear me? Don't drive it until they say you can. No sense in getting yourself arrested for stealing your own car." He laughed.

Ivory nodded emphatically. "Yes, sir, Mister Joe. Yes, sir. Thank you, sir."

"Hold on," I said, fishing the keys from my pocket and tossing them to him. "You'll need these."

He nodded again. "Thank you, mister."

After Ivory left, Joe looked up at us with a I-told-you-so expression on his rotund face. "Now, do you really think that one has the smarts to rob a jewelry store?"

Doreen glanced at me, a self-conscious smirk on her face. I knew how she felt. After the last couple minutes with him, I wasn't even sure Ivory could find the parking lot. Still, Getdown had sent him after Hermie Abraham.

The fat man persisted. "Well? Do you, Boudreaux?"

I grinned. "Doesn't look that way, but then, looks can be deceiving." Joe's brows knit, and I continued. "Now, what about it? Didn't you send Ivory to follow Hermie Abraham?"

He shrugged. "Yeah. I wanted to know where the dude was hanging out. Even Ivory can do a tail. He followed the guy to the Blackhawk Towers. When Ivory come back, he told me the Jew-boy had killed hisself. That's it."

I eyed him narrowly. "You're sure?"

He studied us several moments, and then slapped us both in the face with his next admission. "Listen, Boudreaux. I know you—" He paused and nodded to

Doreen. "And probably your partner is straight up Sherlocks. Fawn okayed you, and that's good enough for me. So, I'm telling you straight. I wanted that skull. I still do, but I had nothing to do with the fire or the old bum's death or the Jew-boy's death. And I sure don't know nothing about no jewelry store robbery. That's serious stuff."

"Why did you lie about going to Dallas?"

He shrugged. "I didn't want no one to know about the skull."

An idea hit me. I glanced at Doreen then fixed my eyes on Getdown. "You say you want the skull."

He looked at me in surprise. "Yeah, but you said it was stolen."

I shrugged indifferently. "I didn't say I didn't know where it was, did I?"

His fleshy forehead wrinkled, and then a devious gleam filled his eyes. "No. I don't suppose you did."

"If I—we—could find it, what would it be worth to you?"

From the corner of my eyes, I could see Doreen staring at me.

Getdown eyed me shrewdly, then glanced questioningly at Doreen. "I ain't lying to you Boudreaux. I ain't sure just how much that Bernard dude will hold still for, but I'll give you a third of what I get from him, which I figure is at least half a million." He tapped the chest of his pale-yellow silk shirt with the tip of a greasy finger, leaving a small grease mark on the garment.

I studied the fat sneak a moment, then nodded. "We'll be in touch."

Outside, we paused on the sidewalk as the late afternoon crowd began to thicken. "What was that about?" Doreen asked, her brow furrowed.

"A shot in the dark. I don't think he was lying about the jewelry heist. He's too eager to get the skull, more than if he had it tucked away somewhere."

She shook her head. "Well, if his Denver alibi holds up, he's for certain off the hook with the fire."

"Could be. We need to contact Bernard."

"What if he lies for Getdown?"

"I don't figure he will. He's one of three world-renowned collectors of the skulls. He's got a reputation to protect."

She cocked her head to one side. "I suppose you heard Buck say he hadn't seen S.S."

It was not a question, but a statement. I arched an eyebrow. "Yeah."

"Could he be lying?" She gestured up the street to Neon Larry's. "The guy up there said S.S. had gone down to the Red Rabbit last Monday."

I grinned. "Buck is the consummate liar. I wouldn't have been surprised when he was born if he didn't try to convince the doc he was girl. He tries to play all the angles."

"What about Ivory? You think he was telling the truth about his Jeep?"

I wanted to believe Ivory. I figured he was one of those poor souls, who, but for the grace of Getdown Joe, would be wandering the streets like Goofyfoot and Pookie. "I'm not sure, but I'd like to talk to him without Joe around, wouldn't you?"

She grinned and nodded to the pickup. "We know where he is."

Chapter Twenty-six

On the way to the parking lot, I called my boss, Marty, who had touched base with one of his contacts at the police station and verified that the Jeep had been reported stolen the previous Monday.

"That don't mean Getdown and Ivory hadn't stashed the car in a garage and reported it stolen," he said.

He was right. That very well might have happened in a situation involving perps with an IQ higher than a re-frigerator bulb, but when one considered Ivory Wash-ington, a gut feeling told you that such a level of deception was far beyond his grasp.

On the other hand, there was Getdown and he was no dummy.

Upon reaching the parking lot, we spotted Ivory Washington speaking with a uniformed officer taking notes while another was climbing out of the Jeep—having dusted for latents, I guessed. I stopped behind a parked car and waited until they left.

As soon as the cruiser drove away, I pulled in beside Ivory and climbed out. Doreen rolled down her window and rested her arm on the sill.

The young man had the door open to his Jeep when he spotted us. He grinned and once again thanked us for finding his Jeep for him.

"Glad to help. And now, you can help us, Ivory."

His grin grew wider. "Yes, sir. Just you name it."

"Remember a couple weeks ago when Getdown Joe had you follow the little man back to the Blackhawk Towers?"

A blank look came across his face, and his forehead wrinkled in concentration. Slowly, he nodded. "Yes, sir. I remembers that one. He was sceered abouts something."

"Joe?"

Ivory shook his head emphatically. "No, sir. The man Mister Joe had me follow."

"What do you mean, scared?"

"He keep looking around and walks fast as he can."

"What happened after he went into the Blackhawk?"

Ivory shrugged. "I gots on the elevator with him and some more people. He gots off on the tenth floor with two other people so I makes like that's my floor and gots off. When I sees what room he goes into, I calls and tells Mister Joe."

"Then what?"

"Mister Joe tells me to wait outside and follow the dude if he goes out, but he never did. Just before the sun done come up, the police come up. I hears later that the little man done kilt hisself." He held his arms out to his side. "I done what Mister Joe tolds me. That's all I knows." He looked hopefully at Doreen and then back to me.

Doreen spoke up. "Ivory, do you know S.S., who works at Neon Larry's?"

His face broke into a wide grin. "Yes, ma'am. I knows him real good."

"You seen him around the last couple days?" She shot me a quizzical glance.

He thought a moment, then nodded. "Yes, ma'am. Him and Bull was in The Lighthouse this morning. Dey was leaving when I comes in."

A shot of adrenaline coursed through my veins. "Bull? You mean Bull Abdo?"

He nodded. "Yes, sir. De laundry man." Doreen and I exchanged smug looks as he reached for the door.

He climbed in and adjusted the seat, sliding it forward five or six inches, after which he tilted the rearview mirror down. He started the Jeep, then his eye fell on an object on the floor in front of the passenger seat. He leaned over and retrieved an Afro wig.

I chuckled. "Nice-looking rug."

He frowned at me and shook his head. "No, sir. Ain't mine." He patted his shiny bald pate. "I likes my head just like this. I ain't got no use for them wigs."

I reached for it. "I'll take it."

He tossed it out the window to me.

After he drove away, I climbed in and tossed the wig on the seat between us. "Ivory's about five nine, wouldn't you say?"

She nodded, perplexed. "I don't follow you."

I explained. "Whoever stole the Jeep was at least six feet or more. I'd guess about six three, and with short or no hair. I'll guess black because of George Sheffield's description. Remember?"

A frown wrinkled her forehead. "Is that what that wig's all about, or are you planning on changing your hair style?"

Laughing, I replied, "Nope. I've been wearing short hair for forty odd years, and I plan on another forty or more. But, I'd give you hundred-to-one odds that's the wig our thief wore last night."

"You really think so?"

"Yeah, and did you see how far Ivory had to slide the seat forward? Almost six inches. And then he had to adjust the rearview mirror. It was set for a tall man."

Doreen thumbed through her notebook. "All Sheffield remembered about the guy was his Afro hairstyle."

Before we could continue our discussion, my cell rang. It was Bull Abdo. He sounded frantic, and he wanted to talk.

"Where?"

"Barton Springs. Thirty minutes."

As we sped toward Barton Springs near the river, I glanced at Doreen. She smiled grimly at me. "What do you suppose Abdo and S.S. have going?"

"Beats me, but I imagine we're about to find out."

Shaking her head, she replied, "Some combination, a bartender and a laundry man."

Suddenly, the nagging thought that had evaded me for the last couple days exploded in my head. "That's it," I exclaimed. "That's it!"

Doreen jerked around, startled. "What? What?"

I tingled with excitement. "The laundry. Something had been bothering me."

"What?"

All I could do was shake my head. "How could I have been so dense?"

"Okay, so you are dense. Dense about what? Tell me!"

I looked around at her. "I know who set the fire."

Her eyes grew wide in disbelief. "What do you mean you know who set the fire?"

Flexing my fingers about the wheel, I nodded. "I know who set the fire. Look in that little notebook of yours to one of our first interviews with Buck. He said something about yellow-and-green uniforms."

She thumbed through her book. Puzzled, she replied, "Here it is. He said 'even fancy green-and-yellow uniforms for my people like Getdown'." She looked up at me. "So?"

"So, how did he know they were yellow and green? The only reason Getdown knew the uniforms were in the back was from the delivery receipt. He didn't even know the color."

Her eyes lit with understanding. "And the only way Buck could have known was the fact he was back there."

My eyes narrowed, and I squeezed the steering wheel until my knuckles turned white. "Buck was in the back room with Rosey."

Doreen looked at me in consternation. "You think that—that Buck—"

Keeping my eyes on the road, I nodded. "That Buck killed Rosey? If he didn't do it himself, he was still responsible."

I could feel my heart pumping hard, filling my muscles with fresh, invigorating blood. I flexed my fingers about the wheel, anxious to finish our talk with Abdo and then get back to Buck Topper.

I clenched my jaw, looking forward to confronting Buck, and then Doreen splashed water on my anticipation.

"I just thought of something, Tony. What if Buck found out about the uniforms from Abdo? After all, he was working for Buck."

Chapter Twenty-seven

Ten minutes later, we spotted Abdo's red Miata sitting in the parking lot overlooking Barton Springs, a natural swimming pool in a limestone basin a thousand feet long and over a hundred wide, fed daily by thirty-two million gallons of spring water bubbling from the underground Edwards Aquifer.

Abdo was sitting on a park bench, nervously puffing on a cigarette. His drawn face was taut with worry, and his eyes quartered the park nervously. He froze when he spotted the pickup, then relaxed and forced a weak grin when he recognized us. His finger was still bandaged.

We climbed out of the pickup and walked across the cracked concrete parking area to him. Behind us, occasional cars and motorcycles passed on the narrow macadam road that twisted through the park.

Despite the cool edge in the air, a few cars were parked along the road or under trees.

"Am I glad to see you." He glanced around nervously. "You've got to get me to the cops. They're going to kill me."

Doreen and I looked at each other, momentarily stunned. I cleared my throat. "What are you talking about?"

He looked around once more, then leaned forward. "Buck and S.S. They're planning on wasting me because of the skull business." A sly gleam filled his eyes. "But, I'll show them. I've still got the skull."

"You what?" Doreen exclaimed.

I broke in. "You're the one who pulled the heist at the jewelry store?"

"Just listen. Okay?" He drew a deep breath, chewed on his bottom lip for a moment, then began. "You know I found the skull at the pawnshop. What you didn't know was Buck sent S.S. to get it that night, but he botched the job."

"S.S. was the one who broke into the pawnshop?"

He paused, sensing my incredulity.

Not too many revelations about the S.S. Thibeaux would surprise me, but that one did. Then I remembered the long sleeve shirt he wore that night behind the bar.

Abdo continued. "Yeah. Got the short end of a dog fight too. Got his rear end tore up and a couple bites on his arm." He chuckled, then continued. "Anyway, we heisted the jewelry store the next night. I waited outside for S.S. When he came out, he gave me the skull, and I hid it, like Buck said. This morning at The Lighthouse, I told S.S. where I'd stashed the skull—Locker 242 at the Greyhound Bus station. He asked for the key, but I'd left it in a safe place. I was supposed to get the key from where I'd hidden it and give it to S.S. later this morning. He wasn't at Neon Larry's, so I tried the Red Rabbit. No one was behind the bar. I started back to Buck's office when I heard him and S.S. planning on wasting me, cutting me out of my share of the skull once they got the key to the locker." He hesitated, swallowing hard. "S.S. asked what if I didn't give them the key? And Buck said he had drugs that would make me do what he said."

He paused, then added, "So, I moved it." He drew a deep breath. "I'm the only one who knows where it is. And now I've got to get to the cops."

"Does Buck know you moved it?"

He nodded jerkily. "Yeah. I called him and told him. I also told him if he wasted me now, he'd never find the skull."

"What did he say?"

Abdo's face paled. "He just laughed. He said he had ways to make me talk." He licked his dry lips. "You see why I got to get to the cops?"

From the nervous shifting of his eyes and constant chewing on his lips, I guessed Bull Abdo was telling the truth. Still, there were a couple holes I wanted to plug. "Why you? Why did Buck have S.S. give you the skull?"

Without hesitation, Abdo explained, "In case the cops

got lucky and collared S.S., he wouldn't have the skull on him."

I arched a skeptical eyebrow. I understood Buck's reasoning although it was a bit dramatic. "What about the diamonds? He give them to you also?"

Abdo frowned. "What diamonds?" He shook his head. "He just had the skull. That's all we was sent there for, the skull."

Doreen looked around at me sharply, and in my head flashed the picture of two open trays in a bank of a hundred trays or so. I nodded slightly, and a knowing smile curled her lips.

In a soft, persuasive voice, Doreen said, "Carlos, we'll take you to the police, but things will go better for you with them if you take the skull with you. You understand?"

He frowned a moment, studying us, then his eyes lit up. "Yeah. I suppose it would. That way, it would look like I was cooperating with them, huh?"

I nodded. "Yeah."

"Okay. Let's go."

"Where?"

A sly grin played over his lips. "It's in the storeroom behind the Hip-Hop. Where the old winos bed down." He chuckled when he saw the frown on my face. "Take off the plate from the light switch and the two bricks below come out. There's a space between the two brick walls. You just slide it out."

I frowned. "I remember the switch, but two walls?"

He grinned. "The place was remodeled twenty years ago. They put in a brick wall on the inside." He grin grew wider. "And guess what I found when I took off the plate? The pawn ticket. Old Rosey hid the pawn ticket behind the switch plate."

I remembered the loose plate. All I could do was shake my head. Doreen laughed softly. "What do you know?" She paused. "One more question before we go, Carlos. You remember those yellow-and-green uniforms you delivered with the laundry on that Monday before the fire?"

He nodded. "Yeah? So?"

She winked at me. "So, did you mention them to Buck?"

"Buck?" He shrugged. "No. Why should I?"

"Just wondering. Just wondering." Doreen looked around at me, a smug smile on her face.

Her smile was dwarfed by the one that leaped to my lips. Like I figured, Buck was the torchman—the one who set the fire and a key player in Rosey's death.

Bull looked from one of us to the other. "So, now what?"

I studied Bull and gave a thankful little prayer for the greed of thugs like S.S. and Buck. Had they not tried to stiff Abdo, they would have the crystal skull in their hands at this very moment. Instead, their world was about to be turned upside down. "Now, we pick up the skull and take it to the cops." I hooked my thumb over my shoulder. "Come on. You can ride with us."

Abdo shook his head. "Naw. I'll go in my car."

With a shrug, I replied, "We'll follow you."

"So," Doreen remarked with a wry touch of humor in her voice as we climbed into the Silverado. "S.S. and Abdo don't do diamonds, huh?"

With a chuckle, I winked at her. "Guess who does?"

She shook her head. "He's a sneaky little creep. How could he figure on selling all those uncut diamonds?"

"Maybe that's the reason."

"What do you mean?"

We pulled in behind Abdo. "They're uncut. I don't know anything about the diamond business, but you can be sure J. C. Towers would not have pocketed them unless he knew exactly how he could get rid of them. He'll clean up two ways, selling the diamonds and insurance." I glanced at my watch. It was almost 6:00. "When we get back to the office, I'll call Chief Pachuca and tell him what we've found about the diamonds. Let them do the legwork."

Austin traffic is always heavy, and afternoon rush hour is doubly so. Abdo drove carefully, observing the speed limit. He pulled up to a signal light at the intersection of Barton Springs and Riverside Drive.

Doreen pointed at Riverside Drive behind us and exclaimed. "Look at that idiot, would you?"

I glanced in the side mirror and spotted a solid black Toyota Supra racing at breakneck speed toward the intersection. Suddenly, smoke poured from Abdo's rear tires. He shot into the intersection, hanging a right and dodging traffic as he headed out Riverside Drive.

"What the—," muttered Doreen.

At that moment, the Supra, its windows heavily tinted, blasted across the intersection in blurring pursuit.

"I don't know," I shouted, "but I'm going to find out." Before I could move two feet, a Budweiser delivery truck pulled in front of me. I looked around frantically, but I was hemmed in on all sides.

"Do something," Doreen shouted, craning her neck to peer over the parked cars in a desperate effort to spot Bull Abdo's red Miata.

"Like what? Last I looked, I can't fly."

The light finally changed, and we headed out Riverside Drive. All we could do at I-35 was peer north and south in frustration.

We were both puzzled and confused.

She scooted around in the seat and frowned at me. "What do you think?"

"Something spooked him."

"The black car?"

I turned left, and accelerated hard. "I don't know, but I want that skull, and now." I reached down and flipped on the police scanner in my pickup.

It was growing late. Locals and tourists were filling the sidewalks on Sixth Street. We parked off Sixth, half a block down from the charred remains of the Hip-Hop, and made our way back to the storage room.

The skull was exactly where Abdo had said. Two minutes later, we were driving away with the Mesoamerican Lemurian Crystal Skull safely in Doreen's hands.

On the way to the office, Doreen asked, "So now what? We wait for Abdo?"

I shrugged. "He's our man. Without him, all we have is the skull."

The scanner was full of the usual garbage, traffic snarls, fender benders, domestic disturbances, a rabid dog, and a missing husband.

Just as we pulled into the parking lot, Doreen grabbed my arm. "Listen."

A call reported a fiery crash involving two vehicles at exit 213 near Kyle, Texas, twenty-two miles south of Austin.

Without hesitation, I made a U-turn and headed south.

A frown knit her forehead. "You don't think it's Abdo?"

Flexing my fingers about the wheel, I nodded. "Could be."

She indicated the exit sign we were passing. "Two thirteen is twenty-two miles away."

"So?"

"Twenty-two miles. We saw them not ten minutes ago. They couldn't have got that far in ten minutes."

I grinned. "Then we'll just be wasting gas, right?"

She shook her head and leaned back.

Naturally, there was a traffic jam. I pulled onto the shoulder and bounced my way as close to the scene as I could. When I saw an officer start toward me, I stopped and climbed out.

He held up his hand. "Sorry, sir. This is as far as you can go."

"Look, officer. If one of the cars is a Miata roadster, I can help. If not, I won't bother you."

He studied me a moment, then waved me forward.

In my business, I've not only seen death, but I've smelled it. And every time I smelled it, I've had to force the gorge back down my throat. That day, the sickening odor lay on the air like a thick fog.

One of the investigating officers came up to me. I told him about Bull Abdo taking off in his red Miata when he spotted a black Toyota Supra coming after him. I played dumb to the follow-up questions he asked, but the fact that he asked them told me I had found Abdo.

Finally, he nodded. "It's them. Both are burned to a crisp. The Supra is registered to S. S. Thibeaux. Know him?"

S.S.? I whistled softly. "Yeah. He works down on Sixth Street at Neon Larry's Bar and Grill."

He jotted the information on a note pad, took my name and number, and thanked me.

The headlights from the oncoming vehicles illuminated the concern on Doreen's face. "So, how do we nail Buck now? Abdo can't testify."

I was stumped. What little evidence we had was circumstantial, and there wasn't enough of it to get any self-respecting cop's attention. "Let's sleep on it. Maybe we'll have an idea in the morning."

"What about the skull?"

"I'll take it home with me and stash it."

In my garage, I had the remains of an old CPU, one of the first computers I had owned. It was about eight inches wide and twenty-four high, a perfect hiding spot.

I removed the outer cover, fit the skull inside, replaced the cover, and went back inside.

At 3:00, the jangling of the telephone awakened me. Sleepily, I mumbled, "Hello."

Doreen's frightened voice jerked me from my sluggishness. "Tony! Buck kidnapped me. He wants the skull."

"What? But—"

"He saw us out at the park with Abdo. He—"

Chapter Twenty-eight

In the next moment, Buck Topper was on the line. "Boudreaux! I want the skull or Doreen here ain't going to be Doreen no more. I want the skull, and I want it now. Meet me at the—"

I interrupted, playing for time—time to think, time to make a hasty plan with the chilling thought that most of my hasty plans had the disastrous results one would expect from a hasty plan. "I don't have it here."

"Then get it. Meet me in the Munkres Parking Lot at six o'clock."

"I told you I don't have it. I can have it by nine o'clock."

Buck cursed. "All right."

"And," I added, "at the Greyhound bus station, second floor by the lockers."

"No way."

"The only way, Buck. I don't trust you." I played a hunch. "You followed Abraham to the Blackhawk and killed him, just like you killed Rosey. There's always a crowd at the bus station. I'm not going to give you the chance of taking us out."

He didn't answer for several moments, then finally, "All right. Nine o'clock. One minute after, she gets it." He paused, then added, "Look, Tony. I don't want to hurt you or the woman. Once I get the skull, I'm gone. You'll never see me again." And then the line went dead.

I studied the crystal skull after removing it from the CPU, wondering just what it was about the object that was so mesmerizing. Could it be true the skull displayed an aura creating energy to some receptive individuals? Was it possible that in the Torah and the first five books of the Old Testament, a code created by a numerical skipping of letters discusses the crystal skulls as my research indicated?

Hard—no, almost impossible to believe. Yet, I had to believe the lengths to which Buck was going to get it.

Shaking my head, I slipped the skull into a Wal-Mart's plastic bag and set it on the table. I planned to arrive early.

The station was on a hill, the first floor opening on to the lower street, the second floor on to the higher street. I chose the second with the lockers. Whichever way Buck chose to leave, first or second floor, we would leave by the other.

At five minutes before 9:00, I spotted Doreen and Buck enter the Neches Street entrance on the first floor and head for the stairs. I glanced around. Half-a-dozen or so passengers were milling about the lockers. I grinned. Too many for Buck to try anything here—I hoped.

While I was angry with myself for letting Buck slip through my fingers, I knew that in all reality, what evidence I had against him would not hold up to the scrutiny of the district attorney.

What I couldn't figure was Buck's move after he got the skull. Would he leave Austin as he said? With three to five million dollars, he could live anywhere he wanted.

As they topped the stairs, Buck grinned. I spotted the bulge of an automatic under his T-shirt. Doreen's features were set. I could see the anger in her eyes, but she kept her lips pressed tightly together.

Stopping several feet away, Buck glanced at the plastic bag in my hand. "Is that it?"

"Yeah."

He started to reach for it, but I took a step back. "Why did you kill the old wino, Buck? He never did anything to you."

He glanced over his shoulder, peering down at the first floor. He sneered. "That was an accident. I tried to get the pawn ticket from him. I slapped him around a little, and he tried to get away and ran into them low pipes in the back room—you know, the ones that go across the hall. I thought he was dead."

"And you set the fire to cover it up."

"So?" He took a couple steps toward me. "Enough of that. Give me the skull."

"What about S.S.?"

Buck sneered. "He ain't no problem no more. He saw to that hisself this afternoon. Dumb jerk." He clenched his teeth and narrowed his eyes. "Now, give me the skull."

"Get behind me, Doreen," I said, keeping my eyes on Buck as I handed him the bag.

Stepping back, he opened the bag and peered inside, the grin on his face growing wider. Slowly, the smile faded as his free hand slid under his shirt and folded around the automatic. "Sorry, Boudreaux, but you two are going with me. I can't afford to leave any unfinished business around when I leave."

Doreen gasped, and I felt her nails biting into my arm. My brain raced. We were too far apart for me to jump him. "Come over here and stand by my side," he ordered us. We did as he said. His hand was under his shirt with the muzzle of the automatic pointed at me. "Now we're going to stroll down the stairs nice and easy. Understand?"

I nodded. Doreen was clinging to my left arm, her nails digging into my flesh. My right was only inches from Buck.

As soon as we took the first step down the stairs, I shoved Buck forward with my right and slung Doreen back with my left. She screamed and fell to the floor. The automatic roared, Buck shouted, the muzzle blast tugged at my jacket, but I didn't plan on waiting around to see what was happening. I spun, yanked Doreen off the floor, and raced for the 8th Street exit.

On the way to the police station, Doreen informed me that Buck admitted that had S.S. not killed himself in the wreck, Buck was going to buy him out of the partnership with lead. "That's when I knew what he had in mind for us."

I nodded.

By 11:00, we'd given Chief Pachuca all of the information we had garnered in the last five days: the fire, the murders. Other than our word, we had nothing to support the admissions that Abdo made were true, but Pachuca did assign a man to prowl deeper into the jewelry heist.

"Towers wouldn't be the first to try something like that," Pachuca laughed.

By noon, we found Getdown Joe, who as usual was gobbling down cheeseburgers in the back of the Red Rabbit. For the first time in my life, I saw him stop eating when we told him who torched his place.

The fat man gulped down half a mug of beer, belched, then said, "You certain it was Buck?"

"Yeah. He told both of us. He even told Doreen he planned to waste S.S., who was also part of the scheme. But S.S. beat him to it when he got himself killed in that wreck yesterday."

He leaned back and glanced at Clay Renfield behind the bar. "What about this place?"

I shrugged. "What about it? Buck won't be back."

A sly gleam lit his eyes. "I don't suppose it would be much trouble for a man to find out, legal like, how to take over something like this when the owner disappears, huh?"

Doreen and I laughed. "I don't suppose it would," I replied.

We went to the office, did our reports, and by 3:30, had cleaned up the case as much as we could.

Getdown was satisfied, Marty was satisfied, Doreen was satisfied, but I wasn't. Buck had beaten the system, and I couldn't do a thing about it.

Doreen and I took the elevator down together. As we headed for our cars, she cleared her throat. "Tony."

I glanced at her. "Yeah."

She hesitated, trying to find the right words. Finally she blurted out, "Thanks for sticking with me. I wouldn't have blamed you for dumping me after those first couple days." She extended her hand. "I think I learned a little about men."

"Or boys." I grinned.

"Or boys." She laughed and leaned forward and touched her lips to my cheek.

I studied her a moment, then hugged her. "We make a good team, partner."

Next morning, I slept late. The telephone awakened me. It was Chief Pachuca. "Well, Tony, believe it or not, Buck Topper turned up at Munkres' Parking Lot, cold as ice. Two bullet holes in the head."

I sat up abruptly, my first thought of the skull. "Did he have the crystal skull?"

Pachuca hesitated. "I guess so. There was a Wal-Mart bag of broken glass beside him. Witnesses said three men wearing suits looked in the bag, shot him, dropped the bag, and drove away. We're checking the plate numbers right now."

"What about the jewelry heist?"

He laughed. "A piece of cake. The one named Sheffield. He broke like a piece of glass. We nailed both of them."

When I replaced the receiver, I stared at the wall, trying to figure out what took place after we left the bus station. Apparently, when he fell down the stairs, the skull shattered.

But, not even Buck was dumb enough to try to pass that off on anyone. All I could figure was that since the buyers were in town, and he had no skull, he was trying to evade them.

Without luck.

They must have caught him at the parking lot.

I lay back and stretched my arms. All of a sudden, the day looked glorious. Strange how when all else fails, Fate sometimes steps in with a helping hand.